JORIE'S MAGIC STORIES

By the same author:

Magic in Fairyland, Book Guild Publishing, 1996

Tales From Magic Lands, Book Guild Publishing, 2000

All at Sea with Rocky and Toppy, Book Guild Publishing,
2004

JORIE'S MAGIC STORIES

Marjorie Holstead

Illustrated by Michael Avery

Book Guild Publishing
Sussex, England

First published in Great Britain in 2009 by
The Book Guild Ltd
Pavilion View
19 New Road
Brighton, BN1 1UF

Typesetting in Souvenir Light by
Keyboard Services, Luton, Bedfordshire

Printed in Great Britain by
CPI Antony Rowe

A catalogue record for this book is available from
The British Library

ISBN 978 1 84624 372 1

*To
Karen, David,
Pamela and Andrea
who gave me the idea for
The Doll's House*

Contents

The Doll's House

When the moon shines in at night,
The doll's house comes to life,
Little folk, so pert and bright,
Dance and play and sing.

Now and then they take the train,
Pack their cases – off they go!
Soon they'll all be back again,
Where they go to no one knows.

Now, alas, the Snows have gone,
The train took them far away,
To where the moon brightly shone
Upon a child, waiting to play.

The moon shed her silvery light over the rooftops, and
gazed in at the attic window. She was amazed at what
she saw, and she smiled as she slowly sailed on her
way around the heavens.

There was such activity in the long dusty room filled
with an assortment of unwanted things – an old vacuum
cleaner, a suitcase or two, a few pictures, a cupboard,
a forlorn and bare Christmas tree and lots of mysterious
bundles tied up in brown paper. Not very exciting you

say. Ah, but what is that perched up high on an old table? A doll's house! Complete with a red roof and chimney stack with two pots made from corks!

A forgotten house. Years ago someone had played with it, moved the furniture around and had lovely tea parties with tiny cups and plates. Now that child must be grown up and off on her adventure of life. With a bit of DIY the house could still be of use to some deserving child, but it was forgotten. No one came up the ladder to look around. The occupants of the house were far too old to climb!

But you would be wrong to think that the doll's house was neglected! Look again! The windows are lit up! It's only the moonlight, you say. Let us peek into the downstairs room – the one on the right of the door. Would you believe it? There's a party going on! Lots of coloured balloons are bobbing on the walls, and just look at the big round table laden with red jellies, mouthwatering pies and a grand iced cake with candles! Can't quite see how many. And people! Yes, real people, not just stiff teddies and dollies, but alive, moving their arms and smiling and talking too.

Will they see me peeping in? I don't think so, this is magic, and they are in a little world of their own. What shall we call them? The Snow Family? Sounds nice and friendly, and comfortable too, don't you think?

Let us join the happy throng, and see what goes on! The little girl is nine today – I've managed to count the candles. What shall we call her? A short name – Anne, Judith? Lets call her Jenny! She's the youngest, I should say, and she has two brothers older than she. Look how

they are dressed! Jenny's party dress is all satin and frills, and the boys have long trousers and white shirts. Mother Snow has a lovely dark green velvet dress with a sparkling necklace, and Father Snow is in his best Sunday suit.

Look, now they are cutting the cake with a tiny silver knife. Will they really eat and drink just like us? Seems so, and how they are enjoying it! The door at the back is opening and in comes a maid dressed in black with a frilly white apron and lacy cap. She's clearing the table.

So what comes next? Mother is seating herself at the piano, and they all gather round to listen. What music is it? I can just hear the faint sound. Ah! I know and love that tune, it's 'The Skater's Waltz'! Jenny catches her brother's arm and they whirl around the table; now the other brother interrupts and takes his turn. What a pleasant sight it all is.

But they are all on the move again and they sit down on the red velvet couch. Father pushes a long coffee table before them and Jenny goes to the corner cupboard. She's bringing out little boards – gosh! – they are all about to play Ludo or Snakes and Ladders!

I look at my watch. Goodness, how late it is, I'll never be up tomorrow. So I leave my post and creep downstairs. The lights are still on in the doll's house, how wonderful it looks in the dark. Tomorrow I simply must visit again, but I'm keeping my discovery to myself for the time being. Besides, the magic might disappear if I bring someone else upstairs. Noiselessly I open my bedroom door and, yawning, I prepare myself for bed.

4

I wake with a start. What's that noise? It's coming from the attic! Will it waken my grandparents? Thank goodness they are a little hard of hearing. I had better go up and see. Cautiously I move the ladder from its niche in the hall and hurry up the stairs. All is dark in the attic, but the doll's house is still lit up.

Mother and Father and children are scurrying about, knocking over the fruit bowl and a footstool. Whatever is the matter? I press my face against the window and there it is – the cause of the commotion. A big moth, frightening everyone as it searches for the bright light.

Oh dear, how did it get in? Down the chimney? Surely not, it's such a big moth to the Snow Family. How shall I catch it? I'll frighten them all to death if I open up the front door – that is, if it opens after all this time.

I know, I'll get the fly spray and squirt it down the side of the door, I don't think it's a perfect fit. Can I get it from the hall cupboard without wakening my grandparents?

I dash down and find the spray, listening at my grandparents' door to see if they are up, but all is quiet and I hurry back. The family are still dashing about hysterically. There, that should fix Mr Moth – and it does. Everyone goes and sits on the couch. Suddenly the lights go out, and it's time for me to leave and catch up on my sleep.

I was late getting up the following morning and my grandparents had already eaten when I put in an appearance. Grandpa was in his greenhouse and Grandma

5

asked me to drive her to the shops, so I couldn't sneak upstairs, though I was dying to see the Snow Family again. What had they done with Mr Moth?

And I didn't go up the ladder the following night. I slept right through till morning.

'Anything you need from the attic, Grandpa?' I asked hopefully.

He gave me a surprised look and said slowly, 'Can't think of anything. It's mostly rubbish up there, John. Have a look round if you like. We've not been up for years. I think your Dad went up for us a few years ago when we had a wasp nest there.'

Alarmed, I said, 'I hope they don't come back again this year.' I was really worried for the Snow Family.

'Oh, all the wasps were exterminated, John,' said Grandpa. 'We had a pest controller man up there.'

I couldn't wait to see the Snow Family again and, unexpectedly, my grandparents were invited out to tea the following day.

'You'll find plenty to eat in the fridge, John,' said Grandma, 'and I know you're good at cooking, so grill a steak or chops if you like.'

I would eat after I had satisfied my curiosity and, having seen my grandparents on their way, I hurried up the ladder.

But there was no light on in the doll's house. All was quiet, the Snow Family sat on the sofa just as dolls, and there was Mr Moth, lifeless, in a corner of the room.

Disappointed, I busied myself grilling a chop and added all the trimmings. Afterwards, I watched TV. So it was night-time when they came alive!

My grandparents stayed out quite late for them, and it was 11.30 when they retired for the night. But I was tired too, and I didn't waken till morning. The following night I decided I simply must visit the attic again as two days later I was going home.

All was quiet the following day and my grandparents went early to bed after their gallivanting the previous day. Would the doll's house be lit up? I held my breath as I stood at the top of the steps. Yes, there it was, all beautiful with its green front door and painted flowers climbing up the wall. I couldn't wait to peep in!

There they were, busily moving around all serene as if nothing had happened. No sign of Mr Moth! I looked at the back of the table, and there he was – how on earth did they get him there? I found a tissue in my pocket and wrapped him up. What were the Snow Family doing now? Mother had moved upstairs to the bedroom above the front door. What was she doing? Taking clothes out of the wardrobe and placing them on the bed. Gosh! Were they going on holiday? She called downstairs and Jenny and the boys came up to the two other bedrooms. They filled the suitcases which were stored on top of the wardrobes.

Oh, this was interesting – where on earth were they going? and more particularly, could they get out of the front door? Of course, that's it, they took Mr Moth out; who else? Father Snow just sat on the couch reading his paper. I wonder which newspaper he reads? Couldn't see the tiny print. Just as I think the packing-up is done the lights go out, and I noticed that I had been happily absorbed for a whole hour. So I shone my torch and carefully went down the steps.

'My, you're a sleepy-head, John,' cried Grandma, bringing me a cup of tea at 9.30 a.m. 'Still, it will do you good having a holiday from your office work.'

Feeling guilty and a bit worried about the Snow Family, I drank my tea. Would they come back to the doll's house? The last night! Tomorrow I was going home. Perhaps I could check up on the Snow Family from time to time when I visited my grandparents, but then I would probably be with Celia. Somehow I didn't think it would be advisable to tell anyone my secret and, after all, the doll's house didn't come alive until the late hours.

I must make the most of my last night. I waited until I was sure my grandparents were fast asleep, then up I went to say my au revoir.

I knew something was different before I took my last step off the ladder. All was in darkness, the doll's house, everything! With fast-beating heart I tiptoed to the house. No sign of life; I shone my torch through the net curtains – nothing! Where had they gone with their little suitcases? Yes, where?

I slowly made my way through the long, low attic. There was no silvery moon to help me. What a lot of unused items hampered my way, and I was so busy watching my feet that I almost missed it. There, underneath the doll's house, was a ruched curtain. Eagerly I pulled it aside. Guess what was there? A steam engine with carriages, green tunnels, signals, booking-office – the lot!

I chortled with relief. I was sure I would find the Snow Family ensconced in a plush carriage all agog for their holiday – to where? I shone my torch, omitting the third class carriages; I was sure the Snow Family would be seated in nothing less than first class!

And I was right, there they were sitting bolt upright with their suitcases on the rack. But no movement. Did they know that I was going away? Did they only come alive for an observer like me? "Bye Mr and Mrs Snow, Jenny and you boys. I'll come again sometime, somehow. 'Bye,' and I climbed slowly down the ladder.

Then came the busy time of my life. I was getting married, leaving my flat and moving into a lovely cottage in the country. Celia and I were delighted to find such a place. It wasn't too far away from my grandparents so we could visit now and again

The Snow Family receded to the back of my mind, but one question kept popping up; how did the Snow Family leave the table and settle themselves in the train?

It wasn't likely I would find myself alone when next I visited my grandparents, Celia would be with me. I still couldn't quite pluck up the courage to tell her; she would be tolerant, I was sure, but would she believe me? I doubted this very much so I kept silent. Life was very demanding and I put it all on hold.

Then, joy oh joy, we found we were to be parents! Immediately I thought of the doll's house, really, yes! After a few years the new arrival would be thrilled to see the Snow Family. I couldn't wait!

The week before the baby was due Celia stayed in hospital. I took the opportunity, between visiting, to pop up and see my grandparents. I stayed overnight at the weekend and I suddenly thought that I would visit the Snows too! We all stayed up rather late but, after I had phoned the hospital to see if Celia was all right, I followed my grandparents and went to bed. I was so tired, but determined to visit the attic when I was sure my grandparents were in the first deep sleep.

Noiselessly, with the ease of practice, I moved the ladder and hurried up.

The moon was full again and the silvery light illuminated the doll's house. It was all lit up! I'd fully expected it to be empty – surely the Snows were on holiday? No, there they were, and they were holding a dance! But this time they were in the bigger room to the left of the door. They had invited friends and all were dressed in satin ball gowns sparkling with beads. The men of course were very smart in evening dress.

I could hear the music, 'The Skater's Waltz' again. Would that I could hear what they were saying! I pressed my ear against the window but just caught snatches of conversation. What a lovely night for dancing, with the moon shining down benevolently. I could have stayed there for ever watching, but I must catch up on my sleep. I wouldn't get much when our baby arrived.

So, reluctantly, I left my post and crept downstairs. Baby arrived the following day; a lovely little girl – just what we wanted – and we called her June.

Now followed hectic months bringing up Baby, working, and doing odd jobs around the cottage. I also spent time with my parents who had come over specially to see Baby. I was really tempted to talk about the doll's house but realised no one was going to be interested while a new live baby was about!

I hugged my secret to myself. Wasn't I lucky? A lovely

wife, baby, parents, good job – and a mystery! It couldn't possibly get any better! Occasionally I wondered – where did all the guests live in the attic? How did the Snows move to and from the train? One day I would find out, but now day-to-day matters occupied my time. June was extremely fascinating, and Celia and I were so very happy.

The years passed in a haze of contentment, and our little baby grew into a fascinating child. Now and again we found the time to visit my grandparents, who were entranced with our daughter. But by now they were extremely old and sadly, eventually, they died.

We were all very sad and realised their house would have to be sold and the contents auctioned. The auctioneers invaded the house, pricing the furniture ornaments, etcetera.

'Anything in the attic?' cried one.

'Nothing,' I replied, hastily, 'just rubbish, but I will clear that!'

'Oh, don't you think an odd-job man could do that, John?' worried Celia.

'No, I'll come over at the weekend,' I spoke firmly and Celia flashed me an enquiring look.

The doll's house! Just the thing for June: I could repaint it and spring-clean everything. Would it still have the same magic? The old excitement was coming back; would June enjoy the same delightful relationship with the Snows?

I couldn't wait for the weekend – to think I had been able to put the Snow Family to the back of my mind all this time! When I arrived, the house seemed so sad

11

and empty without my grandparents; I was by myself, completely alone, but when I carried the ladder to the opening in the attic my depression lifted.

I peeped into the doll's house and there they were, all seated on the red velvet couch. No lights were on – and where had all the dancers gone? I stepped carefully through the long low attic, and opened the dusty suitcases. I found a bundle of papers and some photographs which I placed in my briefcase. The little cupboard didn't reveal anything but a few old mildewed books, They *must* be somewhere but where? I returned to the ruched curtain hiding the train, but the dancers were not on the train.

I looked at my watch, Celia would be wondering where I was and I turned to the doll's house. How was I going to negotiate it down the stairs?

A shaft of sunlight threw its golden light over the floor and I saw the sparkle of a bead – and another bead, leading back to the train! The dancers were not so far away! I felt around the wooden edging on the floor and, at the far side, in the shadow was a little knob. I pressed it, then turned it and it all sprang open. The dancers lay side by side, still glamorous but without the sparkle. I gathered them all up and stowed them away in the doll's house.

With a last look around I headed for the stairs. This was a bit tricky but I took it very slowly and we emerged unscathed in the hall below. It took but a few minutes to put the doll's house inside the car behind the front seats. Goodness! I nearly forgot – the train! I hurried back up the ladder and parted the ruched curtain. I wanted to find a good stout box for this, and I went to the far corner of the attic. The sun was quite bright and I noticed a picture against the wall. Such a pretty picture of a child; funny I hadn't noticed it before. I would mention it to my mother, she might like it. But now I really must make tracks home.

We had a nice big garage cum workshop and I smuggled the doll's house there, throwing a large old sheet over it. Our little daughter was forbidden to enter the garage; nevertheless, I couldn't risk those sharp little eyes noticing things supposedly hidden. All had to be a huge secret until Christmas.

Celia was quite amused that I had brought the doll's house but considered it would keep me happy. She sneaked a look, but by her expression I could see she thought it very tatty and not a patch on the modern dolls' houses in the shops.

Carefully I removed the Snows, the maid and the dancers, and packed them all away in a box. Where should I hide them for safety? I didn't want June to see them before Christmas. By then the doll's house would have a new coat of paint and it would be smartened up inside with wallpaper and a fresh velvet cover for the couch. Should I ask Celia to make new outfits for them all? Perhaps it would destroy the magic? I'd better not risk it. June could ask for new clothes later on if she liked.

So I got to work. First I pulled out the old linoleum which was quite a bit worn. I would substitute carpet from offcuts we had laid in the cottage. The wallpaper was faded; that was no problem, we had small pieces left over which would do. Material for the velvet-covered sofa could come from a discarded dress.

13

When the doll's house was bare it looked so forlorn, and surely no one could imagine that any magic was possible. Never mind, I could visualise the results and this is what banked up my enthusiasm.

I got to work with red paint for the walls, and black paint for the roof and chimney pots, but I used green paint for the front door and touched it up with gold paint round the panels and the letter box. I wondered, then, did the Snows ever get mail? What a thought!

I was delighted with the result and, when all was dry and hard, I tackled the inside. How well it all looked with chequered tiles for the kitchen and bathroom, and flowered carpet on the bedroom, lounge and dining-room floors. The light fittings I washed carefully.

Then I opened the wardrobes. What a lot of outfits! Stacks of suits, gowns and underclothes all beautifully edged with lace or fur. Also, the kitchen had a full complement of pots and pans. What fun June would have, rearranging everything!

When all was finished I called Celia to inspect. 'Oh, it's marvellous, John! June will love it! Now do you think we should reclothe the Snows?

'No,' I said firmly.

'So when are you rehousing the dolls then, John?'

'Not until Christmas Eve.' That was a very special time – a house-warming, if you like – for the Snows.

The run-up to Christmas Day was hectic, and June was full of excitement thinking about Father Christmas and the parties and presents. What *would* he bring her?

But the great day came at last. On Christmas Eve it was quite a business putting June to bed, and several times she came downstairs on some pretext or other. Eventually we tiptoed to her room to assure ourselves that she was, indeed, fast asleep.

'Time for the doll's house,' cried Celia. We carefully carried it from the garage, and placed it on a low chest of drawers just at the right height for her little hands. Then I released the dolls from the box. 'Shall we put in the guests?' queried Celia.

'No, I think not, we'll leave them in the drawer for now.'

'What about the train, John?'

'There isn't room for it here. Let's leave it for June's birthday, we'll think about it all then.'

So the Snows were happily ensconced on the velvet couch, now beautifully restored and the maid stood to one side with her tray. It was late when Celia and I finally made our way to bed.

I couldn't wait to see if the magic was still there and, after I was sure Celia was asleep, I tiptoed downstairs, and entered our sitting-room. There was the dark spicy-smelling tree awaiting its turn of glory with ornaments and tinsel sparkling in the dark. And the Snow Family sat there on the couch, lifeless and unamused.

What a disappointment! I moved the curtains a little, it wasn't a moonlit night. Perhaps that was the magic that made everything work?

I crept back to bed and woke bright and early as June hurled herself onto us with a bulging stocking. Two dopey-eyed parents feigned surprise as she discovered all the treats Santa had left, but they didn't satisfy her for long and she was all agog, and pulled us nilly-willy downstairs to see *the* present.

15

Even the Christmas tree was given a miss as she oohd and aahd over the doll's house. Her joyous cries were all we could have wished, and in no time at all she had reorganised the furniture, and taken Jenny out to show her the gorgeous sparkling tree.

We left her there whilst we prepared breakfast. What a happy Christmas we had. My parents were entranced with their granddaughter and they joined in the games including Mr and Mrs Snow and family. After Christmas, we moved the doll's house into June's bedroom where it had pride of place on a low table containing a drawer just right for the guests!

Last thing at night she made sure all was well with the Snow Family. They were tucked up in bed and the curtains closed. It struck me that even if they did come alive at night she wouldn't be able to see them and, of course, she was always fast asleep. All the same, I took to peeping in her room when we went late to bed, and especially on moonlit nights.

Celia was indulgent, 'Goodness me, John, June will be all right, she will cry out if she's having a bad dream, and we are only a couple of yards away!'

But one morning, around 1.30 a.m., my stomach needed attention. I had eaten too well at a friend's birthday celebration and I needed a tablet. Passing June's door, always kept slightly ajar, I saw the moonlight filling her room. Now was the time, if any, when the Snows would be circulating. I crept in; yes, I could hear 'The Skater's Waltz'! I nearly cried out with excitement, and I put my eye to the window. June had done a fine job closing the curtains, but I could see shadows moving

about. In future I must tweak the curtains so there was an eye-hole for me, but that would have to be after lights out for June.

I could hardly keep the excitement from bursting out, but all Celia said was, 'My, you *are* in a good humour for the New Year!'

So, at every opportunity, I watched for the Snows' magical appearance. What would happen if June saw the Snows cavorting about? We would be in no doubt when that occasion arose!

And it came! Peals of laughter came from her room at midnight. We both rushed in to see the cause of her mirth.

'Oh, Mummy and Daddy, we are watching the dolls in the doll's house – they are dancing about!' Celia and I strode over and drew back the curtains, but all was still and the moonlight showed us the Snows in their favourite stance on the sofa!

June's little face crumpled, 'Now look what you've done! You've spoiled everything – and my friend has gone too!'

Celia soothed her daughter and promised we wouldn't go anywhere near the doll's house at night in future. A woebegone little girl fell asleep, and we felt very guilty.'

'It must have been too much excitement at the fair today, John!'

I disagreed, and I thought tomorrow I would, at last, enlighten Celia about the Snow Family.

Tomorrow came, and June appeared to have forgotten about last night's little drama. She was still busy pulling things in and out of cupboards in the doll's house, and seating Mrs Snow at the piano where a copy of 'The Skater's Waltz' lay.

Celia approached me first about it all. 'Did you hear what June said last night, John?'

'Of course, how could I forget?'

'John, I mean she said "we" and "my friend"!'

I had been mulling it over myself so I was glad Celia led me into my secret. After I had told it all Celia was speechless, then she said, 'Why didn't you tell me before?'

'I was afraid I would spoil the magic, or you wouldn't believe it, Celia!'

She didn't say anything, but she was quite taken with the idea that another child kept June company!

I was thrilled that all the renovations hadn't deterred the Snows from performing their usual programme. But I was too busy with work to concern myself with doll's houses, and so was Celia.

Then out of the blue came a big discovery. There were still boxes to go through from my grandparents' house. One day I was looking at a box of old photographs and I came across one of the doll's house. Then a large photograph of a little girl kneeling by it. Good gracious, it was the girl from the large painting! We'd got it somewhere in our junk room; with Christmas and clearing the house I had forgotten to show it to my mother.

Mother was quite excited when I produced the photographs. 'It must have been my little sister – she died before I was born, so I believe, my parents never spoke of her and I can only conclude they were so upset they moved all her toys up into the attic. We never played with the doll's house.'

I was quite intrigued, and so was Celia. Was the imaginary child who befriended June *that* child? Did she make the magic? I kept my thoughts to myself.

Along came June's birthday, and we titivated the train and its carriages till it was sparkling and ship-shape. Then we set it up on the floor where she could see it first thing in the morning.

We were rewarded by her squeals of delight as she wound it up and, in no time at all, the Snows were ensconced in the carriages on the way to ... where? 'Toot-toot' went the train all morning, and we were sure the family would be dizzy with all the travelling round and round!

Over the years June got a lot of pleasure from the doll's house and the train. New outfits were made for them, and there were occasional repairs to the furniture. The outside walls were repainted, but no additions were made to the family. Apparently they still had their parties and balls, and periodically they went away on holiday ... where? When we went away on holiday, there they all were seated on the couch awaiting our return.

June never mentioned her imaginary friend again, but we heard a lot of talking and whispering on moonlit nights.

As she grew older, June resolutely refused to part with her doll's house, but when she went away on a school trip for over a week, we wondered if the Snows would still have their parties. As it happened, there was one moonlit night, and Celia and I hid behind the door for ages hoping to see the Snows dancing in the moonlight. All to no avail. Apparently they needed June – or someone else?

The years rolled on and our daughter had a boyfriend. A steady boyfriend, and it was serious. Eventually it happened: June was to be married. The house would certainly seem empty without her, but we were determined to enjoy the day and it proved to be delightful.

After it was all over, Celia and I walked slowly up our drive, happy yet sad. It was a moonlit night and the silvery moon smiled in at our lovely cottage. I was tired and the Snows had slipped from my mind. Peeping round the door to June's room I was glad to see the doll's house lit up. How lovely it looked! What a lot of pleasure it had brought! But the curtains were open; of course, there was no June to close them at night now.

The Snows were packing up! I smiled indulgently and watched the proceedings from the chink at the door. They carried their suitcases and trooped out through the front door. I was excited; it was the first time I had seen them do this.

Then amazingly, they disappeared in a patch of silver moonlight, only to emerge seated in the train, suitcases on the rack and ready to go. No one wound up the train, but with a 'Toot-toot' off it went, round and round. I left them to it and went to bed.

The following morning I went in, expecting to see them on the couch, but they were not there. The house was dark and empty. I looked around and noticed the copy on the piano of 'The Skater's Waltz' had gone too. Strange! At first I hadn't realised the train had gone too. Celia and I searched high and low – even in the garden, but not a sign of anyone or anything.

The Snow Family never came back. They had gone

on their final trip. Had they gone to find their little mistress of long ago who made the magic? I'm sure they had.

Christmas Shopping

Jasmine was one of the lovely wood fairies living in the heart of a deep forest. How she loved her home, snugly set in the depths of a wonderful oak tree which had been there for hundreds of years. His thick green mass of leaves made a wonderful canopy in the heat of summer, and the gnarled bare branches supported the snows of winter.

Jasmine loved all the seasons, but best of all was spring, with its carpets of bluebells and primroses.

The wood nymphs had happy days with the fairies, dancing together in patches of golden sunlight or delighting in the crunch, crunch of autumn leaves.

Fairy Jasmine had many friends, but her special one was Lila. On this dark winter's day, just before Christmas, the two had decided to go shopping; they needed to buy presents for their close friends.

Jasmine slid down from her resting-place within the oak tree, and flitted across the forest floor to a splendid beech tree. Knocking gently on the bark she carolled, 'Come on, Lila, it's a nice day for our little adventure! Come along, put on your furry cloak. Let's be off!'

Lila hurried down, looking charming in her white cloak, and carrying a delightful basket made out of straw.

24

The two fairies giggled away when Old Beech enquired where they were going. 'Shopping,' they cried.

'Don't go too far,' he cautioned, 'it might snow. The sky is heavy with warning!'

'Don't you go worrying, dear Old Beech – see you soon!'

Pulling her cloak closely round her, Jasmine led the way ahead. Her fur cloak gleamed in the half-light – such a pretty golden shade. Off they floated through the silent forest. One or two birds marked their progress and a few rabbits scurried away, but the dark day discouraged much activity.

As the trees thinned out, they saw the distant cottages of the little village. They became just a bit nervous – after all, they must now cross an open field.

'All clear, do you think, Jasmine?' The two fairies peered this way and that.

'Think so, let's go!'

Swooping gracefully, they soon covered the distance, and floated towards the village square now set up with all manner of brightly coloured stalls. 'Ooh, how gorgeous!' they both whispered.

Shining Christmas decorations vied with heaps of toys, ornaments and jewellery. Stacks of cakes, biscuits and sweets gave off a delicious mouth-watering smell!

The shoppers were so busy they didn't notice our friends darting here and there. A golden glow came from the lamps, and Jasmine was well nigh invisible in its rays. She had a wonderful time gazing at the glittering brooches and rings – alas, too big for her use. Lila loved the buttons, and popped a few into her little basket, not forgetting to pay with coins she had found among the leaves in the forest.

She too was practically invisible in her dazzling white cloak; she danced among the button boxes and revelled in the happiness of the day. But too soon – someone had caught the shimmer of her rainbow wings peeking out! In a flash a child's hand reached out and held her tight. She wriggled and kicked, but to no avail, and she found herself deep in some recess – and in complete darkness.

Jasmine was bewildered; one moment she was dancing in the lamplight with her friend close by – the next, Lila had vanished, leaving her basket in the thimble-box! Oh, what a to-do! She swirled this way and that, hovering over the boxes far too long – someone might see her!

Jasmine was getting desperate, then she heard a child whisper to herself, 'My very own fairy!' Her little hand strayed to her pocket, reassuring herself that the fairy was indeed there. Jasmine nearly slid in to find Lila, but realised she too would be a prisoner. Nothing else to do until the child and her mother went home. She'd follow them and think up a plan to rescue Lila.

Following close behind, Jasmine saw the cottage but hesitated, better not go in. Lila would be safe with the child; funny thing, she hadn't told her mother! Joanne hugged her secret to herself. Who knows, if Mother knew, she might think the fairy came off the stall! She'd think (oh, dear!) that Joanne had taken it! That would never do!

Jasmine decided to return home and ask for help. She flew sadly through the forest. Was it only hours

ago that she and Lila had embarked on their lovely shopping trip? So happy and full of fun! To crown it all, snowflakes whirled around her, mingling with her tears. Old Oak was happy to see her, but soon lost his smile when he heard the sorry story. He thought long and hard.

'Now you go and warm yourself, Jasmine. Have a cup of nectar, eat some honey cakes. No use *you* getting poorly. I'll give some more thought to this problem.'

Jasmine did as he advised, then hurried to see if Old Oak had come up with a good idea. He had! Good Old Oak! 'It's Christmas Eve the day after tomorrow,' – here Jasmine's tears began again – 'I guess that little girl has a special place for Lila! She'll appear like magic on Christmas morning at the very top of the tree! Then her mummy will accept that Santa Claus brought her, so – no problems for the child!'

'But Old Oak – what do *we* do?'

'Nothing till Christmas Eve! Lila will be quite safe hidden away somewhere. You *must* meet with Father Christmas! I'll find out when he'll be at Rose Cottage, all the trees will pass my message on, then you must take one or two of your friends on Christmas Eve. I think Santa Claus will be able to solve our problem!'

Jasmine found that time just dragged till Christmas Eve. Her friends tried to cheer her up and she went to see Old Beech, who was very upset. She took Lila's little basket which had stayed in the thimble-box, and put it in her home. Then she left *her* Christmas present – a tiny starry button.

But, of course, the night did arrive, and also the snow!

Jasmine and her friends saw the magical forest with unseeing eyes. Silently they flew through the ghostly trees till they came at last to Rose Cottage. Shafts of light came from uncurtained windows. Then darkness as the occupants retired for the night.

But – what was that? A little gleam of light bobbing about downstairs! They all crowded round the window. A child was creeping to the Christmas tree, a little torch clutched in one hand ... and Lila in the other! They all gasped at once! 'Lila, we are here, we're here!' cried Jasmine.

The little girl dragged a stool to the tree; she stretched up to the very top and removed the sequined star. Carefully she wrapped tinsel round Lila and wound it round the topmost branch. The watchers had to admit Lila looked superb, but Jasmine noted the tears coursing down her cheeks.

What was that? The tinkling of bells heralded Father Christmas and his sleigh. 'Heigh-ho, my hearties, what have we here? Pretty little fairies, but all so glum! 'Tis Christmas Eve! I'll soon have you smiling! Come along in! Need any help up to the roof?'

He moved the snow from the chimney-pot then shot down with a plop and a thud! 'Bring me those parcels wrapped in Christmas-tree paper,' he shouted up the chimney, 'and don't forget the one with fairies printed in gold paper.' Santa Claus wasted no time in freeing Lila from her lofty perch. 'Now, now, little fairy, you're all safe and sound and – look! All your friends are here too!'

What rejoicings! And they all helped Santa eat his mince pies and drink his ginger wine!

'But what about Joanne?' Lila suddenly exclaimed. 'She was so kind to me. Gave me chocolate and milk and even cuddled me in her bed. She'll be sad on Christmas morning!'

'I've thought about that,' said Santa as he fixed the sequined star to the tree. 'Joanne has a very special box to open, and guess what's in it?'

'A fairy-doll!' they all chorused.

'Absolutely,' he chuckled. 'Now off we go, it's time all fairies were tucked up in their trees!'

Cherry Surprise

It was a lovely summer's day, and Fairy Violet skipped along happily. Oh, what should she do to-day? She whirled around, her new lilac dress flaring beautifully in the breeze. It was so filmy and gauzy, she *must* go and show it off to her friends up on the hill. How she had searched high and low for just the right material to make this wonderful creation with her own fair hands, and *not* by magic spell!

She admired the harebells and bluebells nodding their heads in time with the fitful breeze. 'Where are you off to, Fairy Violet?' they murmured.

'To see my friends up on the hill!'

'Have a happy time, but don't go near Wizard Waspie's garden will you?'

'Oh, he lives much further up the hill,' declared Fairy Violet cheerily. 'See you later, little flowers!'

She flew off up the steep slope, and came at last to the cluster of mushroom cottages. What a splendid view they must have from their windows! She walked sedately down the path, conscious of the admiring twitters of little birds.

'Hi, Fairy Violet, nice to see you! Come to visit the Blossom Sisters? Hope you find them in,' carolled Gerald Greenfinch. 'I saw Fairy Almond Blossom passing by an hour or so ago.'

'I saw Fairy Peach Blossom passing quickly by a few minutes ago,' tweeted Jenny Wren.

'Oh, bother!' muttered Fairy Violet. 'Anyway, I'll just peek in to see if Hawthorn Blossom or Cherry Blossom are at home!'

'Hawthorn Blossom isn't in,' volunteered Rowena Rabbit, bouncing by. 'You've got to get up very early to catch the Blossom Sisters at home!'

All the same, Fairy Violet tripped on till she came to the pretty mushroom cottage at the end of the lane. A note hung on the door, 'Back in time for afternoon tea!'

Oh dear, what should she do? How to spend the time till then? She didn't want to go back home and set out again; she'd done her morning chores, she was all prettied up in her new dress. Ah well, she'd explore further up the hill! Vaguely she remembered the bluebells' warning, but she wouldn't go anywhere near Wizard Waspie's castle, would she?

She flitted about in a delightful wood. Sally Squirrel looked down from a tree and admired her little visitor. 'My oh my, what do I see? A pretty fairy in a grand new dress!'

Fairy Violet blushed and thanked her sweetly. Poor Sally! She always had to wear the same old sandy fur!

Emerging from the wood she saw, ahead, the gloomy grey castle of the Wizard; lots of turrets and fancy stonework. She'd just have a peep at it. Just one peep! She flew over the high stone wall and held her breath at the sight of gorgeous flower gardens. She *must* see nearer the castle! More pretty flowers, and then lots of cherry trees, absolutely loaded with ruby-red and creamy-scarlet cherries!

Now Fairy Violet was hot and thirsty. Such a long time before she could enjoy afternoon tea! No one was about. No one would begrudge her a few cherries, would they? She flew lightly up to a cluster of gorgeous ruby-red ones, and sank her teeth into the delectable fruit! Oh, that was better! She flew back over the wall and flopped down onto the springy grass.

Finding her way back to the wood, she saw Rollie Rabbit hopping by. 'Hi, Rollie!' He looked around bewildered. 'Hi, Rollie it's Fairy Violet, remember me?'

Rollie stood stock still. 'Can't see you Fairy Violet! Where are you? Hiding behind a tree?'

'I'm right beside you now, Rollie – stop larking about.'

'*You* are larking about, Fairy Violet!'

With growing dismay, Fairy Violet felt her pretty dress. Oh, yes, she could feel it, but not *see* it!

Sally Squirrel heard the commotion, and swung overhead. 'Who *are* you talking to, Rollie?'

'Fairy Violet – but I can't see her. Can *you*?'

Sally peered around. 'Is she playing hide-and-seek?'

Fairy Violet began to cry, 'No one can see me!'

'Oh, dear,' muttered Rollie, 'oh, dear! Come with me – I'll tell everyone what has happened!'

Rollie felt a bit silly talking to no one. His friends thought it all a bit odd and followed him, till quite a trail of woodland creatures turned up at Mushroom Village! Rollie knocked on the front door; the note was still there, but what was that noise? A window opening upstairs! A little fairy peeped out. 'Why, if it isn't Fairy Cherry Blossom!'

'Sorry there's no one at home, Rollie,' she croaked,

'I'm in bed – I've got an awful sore throat.' She caught sight of the woodland creatures. 'What's all this! What has happened?'

'Can't explain from this distance – and you'll catch cold, Fairy Cherry Blossom! Couldn't you let us in and we'll leave a note explaining things to your sisters?'

'Just a minute, I'll put on my dress,' she croaked.

In a twinkling the little green door was wide open. In went Rollie and Fairy Violet – though, of course, she was invisible!

'Your little friends can come in too,' croaked Cherry Blossom, and there was much scraping of feet on the blue doormat! They all stood around looking embarrassed. Rollie couldn't help casting an admiring eye at the pretty room and its comfortable settee piled high with plump velvet cushions.

'Mustn't speak much,' croaked Cherry Blossom, 'or I'll lose my voice!'

'Rightio,' soothed Sally Squirrel, 'we'll give you all the news!'

Fairy Cherry Blossom's eyes flew wide open with astonishment as she heard the amazing story. She contented herself with a, 'Goodness gracious me, where are you, Fairy Violet?'

Fairy Violet spoke from the window-seat. 'Oh dear, Fairy Cherry Blossom, I do hope your sisters can help me. It's not nice being invisible, and I have such a beautiful dress on, new today!' And here her voice wobbled.

'I'd put my arm round you, if I could only see you,' comforted Wanda Weasel.

35

'So would I,' they all chorused.

'I'll just put on the kettle for tea,' Cherry Blossom said brightly. 'Sally Squirrel, will you help me bring in the sandwiches and cakes – they are all ready and waiting in the kitchen!'

Oh, goody, thought Rowena Rabbit. I'm so hungry!

Sally and Cherry bustled about till the table was positively groaning with goodies.

'I do wish my sisters would come home early,' said Fairy Cherry Blossom. 'Poor little Violet!'

Just as everyone had got used to seeing sandwiches and cakes floating to and fro by the window, someone cried, 'They're coming!' In flitted the three fairies, absolutely astonished at seeing their little house crammed full of woodland creatures! Peach Blossom caught sight of a cake floating near the window – and nearly fainted!

'Sit down,' everyone shouted. 'Sit down! Such a to-do!'

'Now let someone be the spokesman,' interrupted Fairy Almond Blossom. 'We can't make sense of all this gabble!'

Fairy Violet spoke up. 'I'd better tell it all quickly, and say that I'm invisible, before you all faint, dear Blossom Fairies!'

You could have heard a pin drop as Fairy Violet told her story!

'Well, well,' sighed Fairy Hawthorn Blossom, 'what will Wizard do next!'

'*Cherries* make you invisible?' exclaimed Fairy Almond Blossom. 'First I've heard of it!'

'And I,' cried Fairy Peach Blossom.

36

'And I,' everyone joined in.

'Perhaps it's only the ruby-red ones that are magic,' spoke Wanda Weasel. 'Perhaps they are some sort of protection for the castle?'

'I don't know about that,' said Rollie, sagely. 'If you didn't let it bother you – you know, being invisible – you could enter the castle without anyone knowing!'

'I bet old Wizard Waspie would know,' cried Fairy Violet, sniffing miserably.

'What about the creamy cherries?' asked Fairy Peach Blossom. 'Did you eat any of those, Fairy Violet?'

'Well, no, they are so near the castle door.'

Little Gracie Goldcrest spoke up. 'I've had a little nibble of the creamy ones – and I didn't lose myself.'

'Well, well,' mused Fairy Hawthorn Blossom, 'that does put a new slant on things!'

'Tell you what,' announced Sammy Squirrel, 'we'll all keep a watch in the trees in Wizard Waspie's garden. We'll go, one by one, when it's dusk, then we'll be there in our hiding-places the following day to see what goes on in Wizard-land!'

'Super idea, Sammy! Will it be too much trouble to have us stay here until it grows dark, Blossom Sisters?'

'Of course not, but Fairy Violet must sleep here tonight in our spare room,' said Fairy Peach Blossom. 'You must be worn out, my dear!'

So Fairy Violet went to a lovely guest-room and Fairy Cherry Blossom went upstairs to bed with a spoonful of honey to soothe her sore throat.

It seemed a very long time for our Good Samaritans before their hour of departure and, one by one, they silently flew or hopped or ran to the Wizard's garden.

Rollie and Rowena Rabbit dug a hole for themselves by the wall. Sally and Sammy Squirrel found a resting-place in the trees where the little birds nested.

'Gosh, I'm thirsty!' moaned Gertie Greenfinch. 'Could just relish a red cherry!'

'Don't you *dare*,' glowered Gerald, 'we don't want any *more* trouble!'

Nothing to see, nothing to report, till late the following morning, just before lunch. Then out marched the Wizard. What an impressive sight! Purple gown reaching to the floor, all embroidered in golden thread, and a skullcap atop his flowing white hair! He roamed the flower beds, and plucked a pure white rose. Then he came their way! Everyone held their breath and froze! Did he know lots of beady eyes were watching his every move? Possibly, but, not by one flicker did his eyes stray to their hiding-places!

He turned to go back into the castle, then, as if it were an afterthought, his hand reached up and plucked a few creamy cherries! A gasp came from the watchers. He stood and ate them, with a slight smile on his face.

'See, I told you *they* are all right, it *must* be the red ones!' exclaimed Gracie.

Sammy had been thinking. 'Perhaps it's not the cherries at all,' he cried. 'Now who is brave enough to eat a red cherry?'

'I am,' tweeted Jenny Wren.

'That's awfully brave of you, Jenny, but you are so small – who knows what effect it would have?'

'I think,' said Rollie Rabbit, slowly, 'that *all* the cherries

38

are OK. Just think – lots of birds pass over Wizard's garden; you're not telling me none of them miss pecking at a juicy cherry, and we've not heard any tales about invisible birds!'

'In that case,' said Jenny, spiritedly, 'you eat one!'

So he did, and his poor wife watched with bated breath as he swallowed the last piece! Everyone gathered round.

Old Wizard, peeping through the windows unobserved, chuckled, 'What a sight!'

As minutes passed, Rollie still stood there as large as life! 'We must hurry back to the Blossom Cottage and tell Fairy Violet,' shouted Sammy Squirrel, 'Come on!'

Peach Blossom was there at the door with Fairy Violet but, of course, no one could see her! 'What news?' she cried. 'Good news?'

Rollie Rabbit reached the door first. 'Depends, depends,' he exclaimed, quite out of breath.

'Come in, come in,' welcomed Fairy Peach Blossom, and in trailed a long line of woodland creatures. Jenny Wren and Gracie Goldcrest brought up the rear.

They all perched on every available seat – the comfy settee, the chairs and the curtain and picture rail! Fairies Hawthorn and Almond Blossom dashed busily about the kitchen and, once more, everyone enjoyed an appetising meal.

'What do we do now?' enquired Fairy Violet, anxiously.

Sally Squirrel looked in her direction apologetically, 'Nothing else to do, but go and see the Wizard.'

'Oh, dear, oh dear,' cried Violet. 'He might turn me into a frog or a spider or...' and she broke down in tears.

'We'll all come with you,' promised Rowena Rabbit, 'don't you fret.'

'He won't like that,' interrupted Fairy Peach Blossom. 'He doesn't allow animals and birds in his castle! But we Blossom Sisters will come with you Fairy Violet. All you creatures can hover in the grounds. If we need you, we can whistle. We have a magic whistle – it doesn't make a sound, but *you* can hear it! Will you bring it from the box upstairs, Fairy Cherry Blossom?'

'When shall I visit Wizard Waspie?' asked Violet when Fairy Cherry Blossom had returned with the silver whistle.

'We will all have a good night's sleep, and then meet up just after breakfast!'

Everyone hurried home to put their affairs in order before night-time.

Fairy Violet couldn't eat much breakfast, she was too excited, but the Blossom Sisters encouraged her to drink a cup of nectar and eat some honey toast.

Then it was time to go. Off they marched to meet up with their woodland friends – their stout allies. They all chattered excitedly till they reached the castle. Behind Fairy Violet came her retinue of birds and animals, subdued now at the prospect before them.

Over the wall flew she with the Blossom Fairies and the birds. The squirrels swung through the trees, and the rabbits burrowed under the wall, followed by Wanda and Wilfred Weasel.

Old Wizard was amazed to see it all happening. 'My, what a lot of friends the Fairy has!'

Coming up to the huge black door, Fairy Violet and the Blossom Sisters quaked in their shoes! Fairy Violet tugged at an iron ring and, immediately, a goblin appeared, all dressed in green and wearing a very disapproving expression.

As Fairy Violet spoke, he jumped a little, but soon recovered and beckoned them into a dark hall. 'Wait here!' After a while he returned and ushered them into a book-lined room where Wizard Waspie sat in state on a carved wooden chair.

'So, you've come at last!' he boomed. 'You are the fairy who stole my cherries!' He looked directly at her and Fairy Violet was suddenly quite sure he really saw her – she was not invisible to him! 'Look what happens when you are naughty!' Fairy Violet shuddered. This was awful, worse than she expected.

'So your friends have come to help you! You're a lucky fairy to have so many! Don't you like being invisible? Can have its advantages you know! But, come to think of it, I don't believe you *are* a bad fairy!'

'Indeed she isn't, Wizard Waspie,' cried the Blossom Sisters, indignantly.

'All right, all right, but don't take my cherries again, do you hear?'

'I won't, I won't,' promised Fairy Violet, secretly vowing never ever to go anywhere near Wizard Waspie's garden again!

'Come over here!' In fear and trembling, Fairy Violet did as he ordered. 'Drink this!' He offered her a tiny glass filled with rosy liquid. Oh, dear, would this make her a frog or a... 'Come along, it's not poison!'

She drank it all up and, even as she drank, her lovely dress appeared, then her wings and, finally, all of her.

42

'My, that *is* a pretty dress. Couldn't see it properly when you were taking my cherries! Now be off with you!'

Goblin Grump appeared like magic and showed them out, Fairy Violet pausing at the door, 'Thank you, Wizard Waspie, thank you!'

All the woodland folk cheered and cheered when Fairy Violet appeared as her lovely, radiant self. 'Come on, let's celebrate at my cottage,' shouted the fairy, pirouetting round and round.

So they all trooped down the hill and crowded into the little mushroom cottage. She sent Fairies Peach and Almond Blossom to the baker's shop to buy delicious chocolate cakes, pies and a big iced celebration cake.

What do you think they *didn't* buy? You've guessed it, *cherry pie*!

Pixie Golf

Perry Pixie put on his thinking-cap. He had just been appointed games organiser, and *that* had brought him problems! Up till now, Pixieland had managed without definite games. Hadn't they enough fun in their lives, what with spells and lovely get-togethers in each other's houses? The days were sunny and bright with laughter all day long.

Whoever had had this new idea for sporty games? Of course, their young new King Julian. He'd got the idea from watching the humans in Mortal-land. Perry could have wished he'd stayed put in Pixieland! What did he want prying into mortal affairs? They were better left well alone, he thought. All the same, Perry was quite proud that he had been appointed organiser.

But now there was a big problem with a game the King had seen and fancied. Humans walked around with sticks and whacked little white balls into holes! The game was very popular. As the King flew over Mortal-land, he could see vast expanses of green everywhere and people walking around with sticks and balls.

Now, it had been a simple matter to fashion the sticks with a flattened wide hook at the end. There was wood aplenty in the forest. Hadn't the pixies got tables and chairs in their toadstool houses? They prided themselves on the quality of their carpentry.

But the problem was – where could they find little white balls? Of course, they would have to be quite small and in proportion to the sticks and their users.

At first Perry wondered if he could utilise fruit and berries, to be found on the bushes and trees. But, one swipe with the stick, and the fruit would squash or totally disintegrate.

He took off his green thinking-cap and sat down outside his mushroom house. It was a gorgeous day but his contentment was marred by the problem on his mind. King Julian was obsessed with this new game – or at least the idea of it.

'What's the matter, Perry?' asked his friend Pip.

'Got any ideas for this new game we're all going to enjoy? I've had the sticks made, they were no problem, but I can't imagine where I will find little white balls!'

Pip sat down beside him, 'I'll have a think too, but my! I'm thirsty, Perry!'

'Oh, awfully sorry, Pip, I'd just forgotten!'

This is serious, thought Pip. Fancy forgetting a glass of nectar on this hot day! Quickly his host returned with biscuits and glasses of nectar on a tray. They munched together in amiable silence.

'When have you to come up with the answer?' queried Pip.

'Well, the King wants to play a game on his birthday, next month. He's already had holes made in that field by Oak Woods.'

'So that's what I tripped over,' exclaimed Pip. 'They're downright dangerous!'

'Oh, they'll be marked with little white flags and the turf smoothed around the holes when all is completed.'

'That's a good thing,' sniffed Pip, 'or half of Pixieland will be hobbling!'

Robin Redbreast hopped by and pecked at a few crumbs. 'Nothing to do, Perry? I thought you would be dreaming up a few white balls!'

'No such luck; wherever shall I get them?'

Robin cocked his head on one side, 'You could make glass ones, I suppose.'

'Oh, too fragile, just imagine splinters of glass all over the place! We'd have the other half of pixies laid-up in their toadstool houses!'

Robin flew away and decided to call on Ollie Owl. 'Sorry to disturb you, Ollie, but my friend Perry Pixie has a problem.'

'Oh, yes, I've already heard about it,' whooed Ollie, sleepily. 'Why doesn't he go into Mortal-land?'

Robin was amazed. 'But the white balls are much too big.'

'I know, I know, but the humans have lots of small objects just the same shape. He's only got to look around!'

Robin flew back to Perry and was only too pleased to relate Ollie's good advice.

'Ugh,' answered Perry, 'can't say I like Mortal-land. Nothing but trouble seems to come from there.'

'It's worth a try, Perry,' murmured Pip. 'Supposing I come along too, we'll make it a lovely day out!'

With a bit of persuasion, Perry was ready to embark on his quest and, the following day, with haversacks on their backs, they flew out of Pixieland.

48

Robin Redbreast chirruped 'Good luck' as they flew through the woods and out over open country.

'Plenty of green fields here, Perry.'

'Not for playing golf, Pip. When we see villages, that's the time to look out for golf courses!'

Sure enough, when a church spire and a farm or two appeared our friends found what they were looking for. Swooping lower they marvelled at the sight of men walking about with sticks and hitting white balls far and wide.

'I can't see why the King wants us all to play this silly game,' grumbled Perry.

'Well, he does, so we'd better concentrate on finding him some balls to hit!'

'Hey, there goes one ball into that copse of trees. Let's dive!' Perry became excited now that he could do *something*!

They looked in dismay at its great size. 'What did Ollie say, Pip? Look around in Mortal-land and the humans have lots of things that will do!'

'Quick,' warned Pip; 'here comes the man after his golf ball!' They soared high in the air, just in the nick of time.

'I guess it's time to don our invisible cobweb caps,' enthused Perry. 'Let's alight at the top of that hill and have some refreshment too.'

So, after they had rested and donned their cobweb caps they sallied forth into the village. Pip found it all very thrilling to mingle with the shoppers in the High Street and soon Perry was caught up in the drama of it all. What *would* the humans say if they could only see them, but they were able to see one another!

It was absolutely riveting to gaze into the shop windows

49

and wonder and exclaim at the variety of things for sale. Up and down they flew and even ventured inside the shops! What was so awful about Mortal-land? thought Pip. It was so exciting!

But though they looked in shop after shop, admiring the big cakes, the enormous flowered hats and dresses and the wonderful china cups and saucers, they didn't see any white balls!

'Let's go and see what this little boy is buying,' whispered Pip.

The window was cheerily decorated in pinks and yellows with fluffy chicks and shiny foil-wrapped rabbits. As soon as Pip and Perry got into the shop, they were spellbound at the sight of large glass jars ranged on shelves round the walls. A myriad of brightly coloured sweets delighted the eye – caramels, boiled toffees, dolly-mixtures, cherry lips, coconut squares, chocolate raisins, and goodness knows what else!

'Oh,' they both cried excitedly, 'what wonderful sweets!'

'But are any round and *hard*,' Pip said sharply. 'They'll be just like berries and squash!'

'Oh, don't be so pessimistic,' cried Perry. 'I'm sure we will find something we can use!'

The little boy was clutching his pennies in his hot little hand. 'Four pence of Liquorice Allsorts, please.' The lady weighed them out and a mouth-watering scent pervaded the shop.

'What delicious-looking sweets!' Perry exclaimed. 'And what pretty colours, pink, black, yellow and white.'

The boy took the bag and stowed it away into his blazer pocket. 'Is that all, Eddie?'

'No, Mrs Jones, I think I can just afford four pence of aniseed balls too!'

She weighed them out carefully in the shining brass pan, and Eddie quickly popped one into his mouth.

'Just the thing, Perry! If only they were white!' Do they *have* to be white? wondered Perry.

'Mind you don't swallow one,' warned Mrs Jones. 'They're hard.'

'I know,' said Eddie, 'but they last for simply ages if you suck them!'

Our two friends were beside themselves with joy. Now what must they do? Wait, of course, for nightfall. They could enjoy themselves in the town or ride on one of the big red buses, but supposing Mrs Jones shut up her shop before they got back?

So they contented themselves with perching on a stool and watching the customers. They helped themselves to bits of toffee stuck on the weighing-pan and declared it delicious. But that made them thirsty, so they decided to explore and floated into the room at the back of the shop. Sure enough, there was a small kitchen and a sink, of course, with taps. But they couldn't turn them. Pip spotted an enormous tea-pot and he gingerly removed the lid, but only soggy tea-leaves were left. As if in answer to their prayers, Mrs Jones came hurrying in. She filled the kettle and rinsed out the teapot, then she brought milk from the fridge and poured it into a yellow milk-jug.

'Come on Perry, a drink at last!' The two drank deeply from the jug. What *would* Mrs Jones have done if she had seen two pixies drinking milk in *her* kitchen!

51

But she didn't – she just added more milk from the fridge!

What a long time before Mrs Jones locked up the shop and pulled down the blinds. At last our friends could look round the shop and peep into tins and open jars – if they could! Supposing the lid wouldn't unscrew for them on the jar containing the aniseed balls! But with a hefty push or two it came off, They wasted no time in scooping the sweets into their haversacks. What a hefty load to carry back to Pixieland! Pip dropped one and it rolled from the counter onto the floor. Quite a good test – the aniseed ball didn't break.

Mission accomplished, the two pixies sought a bit of fun. They bobbed up and down on the scales and enjoyed it immensely till the door opened and Mrs Jones stood there. She gazed in amazement at the swaying scales, shook her head in wonder and picked up the aniseed ball from the floor. Would she put it back in the jar? Certainly not – she was a very responsible woman *and* keen on hygiene!

Perry breathed a sigh of relief. No doubt she would notice the level of aniseed balls had dramatically fallen when next she sold them; she would really think her memory was failing!

Pip was anxious. 'What can we give her in return, Perry?'

'Oh, don't you worry about that, Pip. I've brought a four-leaf clover!'

'A four-leaf clover?'

'Yes, it will grant one good wish!'

'Let's hope Mrs Jones doesn't wish for anything silly!'

When the door was unlocked, early in the morning, Pip and Perry danced out of the shop. They cast one last look at the four-leaf clover sitting in the jar of aniseed balls, then off they flew. The haversacks were heavy but they themselves were light-hearted!

'I'd like to see her face when she sees the clover-leaf,' chuckled Perry.

Over the hills and dales they flew, through Oak Woods and into Pixieland. Just for a few minutes they floated down to watch the golfers.

'Does King Julian know how the game works? Does he know the rules, Perry?'

'What a thought!'

Maybe they would have to haunt the golf courses till they knew all about the game!

The King was delighted with the aniseed balls. He would have preferred them to be white, but he contented himself with asking the chief painter to dot them with a white spot so they could more readily be seen!

What excitement when the first golf tournament was arranged, but before then, Pip and Perry returned to see if Mrs Jones had had her wish granted. They flew down the High Street to the sweet shop – but it was empty!

'Oh, Pip, what has happened? Mrs Jones and her shop have disappeared! Has she gone to another country?'

Just then two little girls skipped by. 'Let's follow them,' suggested Pip. 'See, they have pennies to spend!'

Sure enough, they stopped before a grand new sweet-shop. They gazed with wide-open eyes at the luscious window display.

'Oh, look Pip, there's Mrs Jones inside. She wished for a lovely big shop! Let's be off!'

'Just a minute, we must see if she's got any more aniseed balls!'

They flew in with the next customers – and there on the shelf was a big jar full of aniseed balls. But what was really eye-catching was a bright green clover leaf painted on the front!

Breakfast with Fairy Bluebell

Fairy Bluebell was a lovely little fairy. All dressed in a heavenly shade of blue she flitted around Fairyland helping her sisters sort the different berries and, in the evening, she closed the petals of the buttercups, daisies, clover and bluebells. How happy she was with this routine and then, oh wonderful day, she came of age and was allowed out in Humanland!

Her elder sisters cautioned her about the perils in this new world, and there was a list of things to avoid. She listened carefully, and vowed never to flout this good advice.

All went well for a year or more, and she didn't put a foot (or a wing!) wrong. As a matter of fact, she didn't consider Humanland anywhere near as wonderful as Fairyland.

But, one day, on an excursion there, she found something really, really interesting! She forgot, momentarily to obey the golden rule – don't stray or stay anywhere you don't understand. Keep well clear!

She came across this gigantic building. How vast it was, with lots of windows showing people inside doing things she couldn't begin to understand! She turned to go but caught sight of something fluttering on a window. Oh, dear! A butterfly with its wings caught by a spider's web. She hastened to release it with one swipe of her wand.

'Oh, thank you, Fairy Bluebell, thank you!'

'Keep out of the way of spiders, little butterfly, and don't go near windows.'

Little Miss Butterfly fluttered off nearby to rest on the weeds surrounding the factory.

Fairy Bluebell should have followed her own good advice, but her attention was caught by the sight of dozens of little people all piled together in a big box. She pressed closer to the window. Humans were popping them into enormous boxes further down the line, but first they shrouded them in plastic. Oh, how awful!

Were they people? Surely not! Fairies then? No, they hadn't wings nor did they carry wands. But some were carrying things at their side! All were dressed in brightly coloured clothes. Were they alive?

She slid up to the top of the hopper window, but found it too slippery and oh, horror of horrors! She found herself sliding down and down till she fell in a heap on the factory floor!

She lay there absolutely deafened by the noise; her little heart was beating crazily. When all was quiet she'd fly up to the window and never, ever come near this place again!

But Lady Luck was definitely not on her side that day; a massive foot lumbered by threatening to squash her. She just managed to roll out of the way – but then the foot stopped. 'What's this toy doing lying on the floor?' An awfully big pink hand reached out and scooped her up!

58

Fairy Bluebell held her breath, she must keep quite still, that she knew, or otherwise she'd end up in a museum! 'Hmm, haven't seen this type before – quite pretty. Here, Madge, you've dropped one of your toys!'

Madge grabbed Bluebell and pushed her into a plastic envelope – and stapled her in! Not a second look did she give! Madge was concerned with what she should feed her family this evening! 'Pizza and chips again? Sausage and mash?'

Little Bluebell sailed on her way on the conveyor belt. Madge's friend, Pat, scooped her up and pushed her into a massive box – not empty but packed with crackly bits, raisins and, joy oh joy! Bits of nuts! Fairy Bluebell was hungry, she must keep her strength up.

Now to get out of this plastic overcoat! She attacked it vigorously with her wand, and breathed a sigh of relief when it fell off and she could enjoy her almond nuts! She wished the box wouldn't keep bouncing up and down as it moved along the conveyor belt – she couldn't enjoy her meal to the full!

After a time she felt a different motion. The box moved up and, with a jolt, was pushed again to lie, at last, perfectly still. Whatever next? Fairy Bluebell settled herself for the night. Mustn't worry – she needed her sleep. She would think about what (if anything) she could do on the morrow.

Tomorrow came (she guessed) and she and the box once more bumped and shook for what seemed like years! Then an uplifting movement again, and finally lying still somewhere.

'Oh my, music!' Fairy Bluebell was quite amazed. She

heard muted voices and the clump of passing feet. Oh, if only she could peek out! Fairy Bluebell was in a supermarket! How long would it be before someone took the box home? She guessed she would have to start eating the crackly bits eventually! Fortunately her box was at the front of the pile, and once more she was shaken about and taken on a bumpy ride.

Oh, dear, she had eaten nearly all her favourite nut pieces. She tried one of the crackly bits and found it quite to her liking! What would happen next? She spent another night with her head pillowed on some nice plump raisins!

When Fairy Bluebell had finally given up hope of ever seeing daylight again – the sound of voices! Then a sudden tearing noise; the box wobbled and – hurray – the light flooded in!

She was totally unprepared for what happened next. She suddenly felt herself swept along, willy-nilly, with the raisins, nuts and crackly bits. With a mighty whoosh she landed in a heap in the middle of a bright yellow bowl. Horrified, she looked up to see a massive jug overhead and a stream of milk threatening to drown her!

Just in the nick of time, a child's voice cried, 'Stop, Mummy, you're drowning my lovely toy!' The child rescued her from the soggy flakes and waved her aloft triumphantly. 'It's a fairy, it's a fairy!'

She smoothed out her crumpled gauzy dress and straightened the jewelled wand. 'She's a bit wet, Mummy.'

'She'll soon dry out in the sunshine. I'll put her on the window-ledge.'

It wasn't long before the little girl, Penny, took her

61

away to play in her doll's house. What a happy time they had! All kind of games they played, from being cook in the kitchen, watching TV, and finally to bed in the white-painted cot. Then Bluebell was left alone. She hadn't had time to think what she should do next. She had been too busy!

After a while she plucked up courage to leave the doll's house. She marvelled at Penny's pretty bedroom, but soon flew to the window. How high up they were! She looked down into the garden, with lovely flowers and some brightly coloured objects she couldn't understand – a swing, a paddling pool and a slide.

Why, there was a bird drinking from a little glass pot – looked remarkably like Tommy Thrush! A butterfly or two danced by and Bobby Bumble-bee! Oh, she must join them! But the window was tightly shut.

She sank down on the window-ledge feeling very sorry for herself; she was hungry and very thirsty. She looked around but there was no sign of any food. She'd tried things which looked like food in the doll's house, but it was only horrid stuff like the plastic overcoat!

Night time came and, by then, she had flown back to the doll's house. Her considerate mistress came to tuck her up for the night and kiss her good-night; in spite of her worries, she slept.

Morning came. Oh, she did wish Penny would take her down to breakfast! How faint she was! How low she was feeling.

All was quiet today after someone came to make the bed. She lay on the windowsill. Even if the window had been open she couldn't have flown up to the little window above.

She was feeling very sad when she heard the door open. Oh, what would Penny have said if she could see her now – out of the doll's house all on her own! But it wasn't Penny. The lady opened the window, not even bothering to put Bluebell back in the doll's house. Now if only she could get something to eat to give her strength!

Minutes passed by and then – buzz, buzz! Who was that? Someone she knew? Her heart lifted with happy anticipation. A big, furry body plopped down beside her. Bobby Bumble-bee!

'Oh, Bobby how glad I am to see you!' A tear or two rolled down her cheeks.

'Now, now Fairy Bluebell, it's all right, I've come to rescue you!'

'How did you know I was here?'

'Sheena Butterfly – you know, the butterfly you released from the spider's web – stayed a while that day and saw you fall into that big building. She saw you on the floor and then put into a big box! Everyone's been awfully busy. All the fairies have been following the boxes to see where they were heading. The birds, the bees and the butterflies have been peeking in windows all over this village!'

'Ooh, I'm so glad,' cried Fairy Bluebell, 'but Bobby, I can't fly, I'm too weak!' and she sobbed bitterly.

'Not to worry, little fairy, I'll carry you out into the garden, then I'll buzz off to find some food for you.'

Fairy Bluebell and Bobby flew to the top of the window. Oh, how fuzzy and warm was his coat! Fairy Bluebell felt better already! They sailed down into the

garden to the appreciative tweets from the birds. 'Here, stay under this rhubarb leaf till I return!'

How lovely it was to be outside! Fairy Bluebell soon regained her strength when Bobby plied her with honey from the hive and long drinks of nectar.

Tommy Thrush came tip-toeing by to see if he could offer a lift to Fairyland.

' 'Bye Bobby Bumble-bee, 'bye Sheena Butterfly, 'bye all you dear kind friends! I'm having a party on my birthday on the eleventh and you are all invited!'

And what about Penny? Did she wonder where Fairy Bluebell had gone? Not really, for before long Mother opened a new packet of muesli. She hoped this new packet would contain more nuts. The last packet was decidedly short of them! There she found a new Fairy Bluebell!

When the supervisor picked Fairy Bluebell from the floor she wondered about this new toy. She made enquiries – no, it wasn't a new design. Where on earth had it come from? But, with her help, a new design was created to delight lots of little girls in Humanland!

The Magic Tree

Once upon a time, the little people of Jelliland were wakened up one night by flashes of lightning and rumblings of thunder.

'Gosh, that was bright,' said Perry Pixie sitting up in bed, quite a bit alarmed.

But the storm was brief and all the pixies and fairies went back to sleep. How amazed, therefore, they were to find a big tree, fully grown standing in the market square as if it had been there all its life! 'How did *that* get there?' they cried. 'Perhaps the storm brought it!'

The magical tree spread out its branches, providing welcome shade in the heat of the summer, and little birds made their nests in the leafy branches.

The little elves made a grand circular seat, and then painted it a lovely green and everyone said what a wonderful present the tree was for them all.

'Let's have a party on Midsummer's Day,' boomed the Mayor of the town.

'Yes, let's,' echoed all the fairies and pixies.

There was such a baking in the kitchens and such a running-up of rainbow-hued shirts and dresses, for they all wanted to look their best on the great day.

As the day approached there was very little left to do. Lots of tiny tables and chairs were delightfully positioned around dear old tree – though really it wasn't old, was it? Cups and plates with matching serviettes in blue, yellow, red and green were lovingly set. Inside the kitchens jellies were made all ready for the morrow, and all kinds of cakes and biscuits. The sandwiches were to be cut fresh on the day.

Perry Pixie sat on the circular seat alongside his pal Pinkie. 'My, that was hard work, but worth it, I should imagine, for the fun we'll all have tomorrow.'

'Oh, yes Perry. Do have a cup of nectar, it's rather special – I've added a tang of lemon.'

'Thanks, Pinkie, it's delicious.'

The two friends sat in silence in the dusk of the evening and idly looking up at the magical tree. Perry looked thoughtful, 'Have you ever wondered where the tree came from Pinkie?'

Pinkie looked surprised, 'Well, I did at first, but it's ours now, and it's such an asset to the town, we would be lost without it.'

Perry sipped his drink reflectively and he sighed. 'I wonder why it came, Pinkie?'

Pinkie chuckled, 'You do bother about things Perry. Come on, you're tired, it's time for bed.'

Perry woke up the next morning and stretched luxuriously. On the chair was his smart new yellow outfit, and he couldn't wait to try it on! The room was filled with golden light, how peaceful everything was, very peaceful. It must be really early; no twittering of birds. He had grown used to their carolling every morning. Reaching over to his dandelion clock he stared in amazement – it was only four o'clock!

He sat up and leaned over to the window; strange, he could usually see the branches of the magic tree gently swaying in the morning breeze. He sprang out of bed and rubbed his eyes in disbelief; the tree had gone! What a shame! The tree, their magical tree had gone, where? The square looked so forlorn and empty, and where were all the birds?

Amazing, too, the circular green seat was still there and, of course, the tables and chairs. But today was Midsummer's Day, the day of the party. He'd run over to Pinkie's house to share the news. On second thoughts, better not, he would have breakfast first. All the same, he really couldn't concentrate on that simple task and he forced his meal down.

Then, running to his front door, he spied his neighbours. With a rush they all darted over to where the magic tree had stood.

'Oh, look, not one leaf is left,' mourned Fairy Lilac.

'There's not even a hole,' exclaimed Woody the Elf.

Pinkie, all sleepy, stood bewildered, looking at the empty space. 'Did you hear anything during the night, Perry? Your house is nearer than mine.'

'Not a twitter or a creak,' said his friend. 'I slept as sound as a bell.'

'It's no use standing about,' cried the Mayor, resplendent in gold pyjamas. 'We must all set to and have our party just as if the magic tree was here!'

'The birds have gone too,' piped a little pixie. 'They won't need my breakfast crumbs,' and he burst into tears.

Slowly everyone tackled their jobs, but the joy had

gone out of it all. As the day progressed, the sun grew hotter and hotter. 'Oh, for the shade of magical tree,' they mourned. Nevertheless their faces brightened as tables were piled high with delicious goodies brought by the fairies in charming flowered aprons. The elves and fairies recovered their appetites and, afterwards, they all joined in the games and maypole plaiting.

It was only as evening approached and they sat together on the circular seat that nostalgia set in. 'It's not the same,' pouted Fairy Rose, 'Where oh where has the tree gone?'

Slowly everyone went home to their toadstool houses, secretly hoping magic tree would miraculously return on the morrow. But morning came, and no tree!

Perry joined his pal, Pinkie, for elevenses. 'Any ideas. Pinkie?'

'No,' said he sadly. 'Thought the Mayor might have come up with an idea or two.'

'A bit early yet, but he should call a grand general meeting and pool all our suggestions,' rejoined his pal.

They didn't have long to wait. Out strode Melvin the Mayor, gorgeous in a purple tunic which showed off his long white beard and curly hair. Everyone poured out of their homes and sat around or sprawled on the emerald grass.

'Ahem,' he said, fingering his beard. 'We are all mourning the loss of our beloved magic tree. We are reminded today of just how magic it was (here he hastily amended, it is.) Has anyone any suggestions, any at all, as to how it may be recovered?'

Apart from setting out to find it, no one had. Supposing

they did find it, how could they bring it back, it was such a magnificent, fully-grown tree.

'As we miss it so much, let us plant a new one,' cried Fairy Lilac.

'Silly,' said Pinkie, 'it would take ages to grow to the, size of the magic tree.'

Fairy Lilac blushed, but Fairy Rose rebuked Pinkie. 'And what, may I ask,' cried she, 'is your solution, Pinkie?'

Pinkie coloured, and mumbled, 'I must think about it.'

'Then do that,' replied Fairy Rose crisply.

The grand meeting was over. Pixies and fairies wandered off in all directions, to find the tree.

'Seems a daft idea,' sighed Perry, 'but what else can we do?'

'Let's have lunch here and take a picnic this afternoon,' suggested Pinkie.

So they did, and set out with some sandwiches and fruit along with two little cups to dip in a clear stream to quench their thirst.

Pixieland wasn't very big, but they soon found out it was quite big enough for them, on foot. Uphill they trudged passing many pixies and fairies coming back home, tired out and weary.

'Surely,' someone said, 'if the tree was anywhere we would have seen it from the top of this hill!'

'Quite right,' agreed Perry seriously to his pal, 'but let's go on Pinkie. Ours is a magic tree – it might not abide by the rules!'

So they journeyed on till they were quite alone. Ahead

rolled the purple hills marking the border between Pixieland and Wonderland.

'Seems an awful long way, Pinkie,' puffed Perry. 'Shall we turn back?'

'No, let's go on.'

Night was drawing in as our two adventurers came to the gates of Wonderland.

'Hi, there,' shouted an official all clad in blue. 'Where are you two going so late in the day? Have you got a pass?'

Pinkie and Perry quaked in their shoes. Falteringly they said, 'We didn't know we had to have one, and we've come a long way, right from the Town Square in Pixieland. We've come to find our tree!'

'To find your tree?' laughed Pixie Wonder. 'What does it look like – a tree?' Then, more kindly he said, 'Take your pick, travellers, but I doubt it will walk away with you,' and he laughed again.

'That way,' he pointed upwards, and our two friends walked slowly up a winding path. There a notice said 'Toadstools to rent for the night.'

Pinkie shouted with relief, 'Come on, Perry, let's have one of these and start our search tomorrow!'

A smart pixie, also in blue, showed them round a lovely cream and green dwelling, and thankfully they threw themselves down on mossy seats, and ate their picnic. No sooner had they eaten than they fell asleep, exhausted by the day.

When Perry awoke he thought at first he was at home, till he saw Pinkie fast asleep in his comfy bed. Perry peeped out of the window; all was quiet. He tiptoed over to the back window and saw, with delight, trees in the distance. Was magic tree one of them? He couldn't wait to find out, and was glad when Pinkie stirred, and he could tell him the wonderful news.

'Are they all magic, Perry?'

'Don't know, but what if our tree was the only one to go gallivanting about. Let's go and see!'

With light hearts they journeyed towards the woodland, eating fruit on the way by way of breakfast. Soon they were under its shady canopy, listening to the sweet sound of birds carolling their joy at living in such idyllic surroundings. All around was cool and shady with the tall trees sheltering them from the sun.

'Dear me,' whispered Perry, 'how on earth shall we find out which is *our* magic tree?'

'Goodness knows,' whispered Pinkie. Then, 'Why are we whispering, Perry?'

He laughed and said, 'It feels just like entering a cathedral!'

'Let's sit down for a minute and think, Perry; I can't imagine how one of these trees could suddenly uproot itself and wander off, can you?'

Perry shook his head. 'Mind you, the tree was uprooted on the night of the storm, but there wasn't a storm in the early hours of Midsummer's Day.'

'That's true,' agreed Pinkie. 'It's all very confusing!'

After a while they decided to retrace their steps and go home. They had eaten all their fruit, and they wanted to be back home where all seemed so friendly and their homes were the last word in comfort!

'We've come a long way for nothing,' mourned Pinkie.

'We will have to put something else in its place – like a maypole.'

'Oh no you won't,' grunted a voice up above.

Where on earth was the voice coming from? Their magic tree had never, ever spoken to them! Way over to the left they saw two trees very close together, exactly like their magic tree.

'Did you hear that, Perry?'

'Oh, yes, Pinkie, oh, yes!'

They scrambled over the root-strewn floor till they halted at the foot of the trees.

'Are you our magic tree?' they both gasped in delight.

'We're both magic trees,' boomed he. 'Have you room for two magic trees in your square? I couldn't stand being parted from my lady love. The storm uprooted me and she was left behind. So I left you on Midsummer's Day for that is the day when my magic works, you see. My love had no idea where to search for me. I'm sorry I spoilt your lovely festivities!'

Perry and Pinkie were spellbound, here they were talking to their magic tree; what a tale to tell their friends!

But suddenly they realised – the tree's magic only worked on one day of the year!

As if reading their thoughts, the tree spoke again. 'Can you wait so long?'

'Yes, oh yes,' they cried. 'Of course, we have room for two magic trees, we will set to work straight away and put a new painted seat round your lady. What colour would she like?'

'Blue,' she whispered shyly!

'We will come and visit you from time to time,'

75

shouted our two pixies, 'and what a fine Midsummer's Day we will have next year!'

What a triumphant two arrived back in Pixieland – Jelliland, I should say! Everyone set to work at once to beautify and make way for two magic trees. They repainted the green circular seat and made a lovely new blue one. Excitement grew, for they were all deciding what new dresses and shorts they would wear and what kind of food they would bake!

At last the great day arrived, but no one got any sleep that night; they all wanted to see the magic trees' arrival. Strangely, no one did, but wasn't that all part and parcel of the magic?

So, how did the trees become magic? Ah, well, that is another story!

The Wizard and the Witch

Wicked Wizard sat in his gloomy castle and wondered what to do about his arch-enemy Witch Wacky. She had scored another victory over him. He had come home to find that she had sneaked in through the shuttered window of his bedroom and filled his bed with blackberry thorns. Cunningly she had strewn them beneath the sheets at the foot of his bed. He rubbed his tender feet with salve – they were still sore. Wait till he could think up a good reprisal.

The culprit, Witch Wacky, was crooning to herself as she stirred her black pot of meat and vegetables over the glowing fire. Every now and again, she tee-heed as she thought of Wicked Wizard springing into bed last night! All the same, she had better watch out; he was certainly going to get his own back very soon!

That night she sailed over the wooded countryside on her sturdy broomstick. The moon was full and shed its light over the ancient castle. How impressive it looked, and so unassailable. She cackled to herself, remembering how she had used her mother's special spell to unlock the shutters to Wizard's bedroom windows. How he would wonder how on earth she had got in! Closing them again after her naughty deed had been another marvellous idea!

What could she do on this lovely moonlit night, she wondered. Might she visit her sister over the hills? No, she didn't fancy a long flight, she would just cruise around.

Goodness, what was happening over at the castle? What could Wizard be up to? All his retinue of servants were lining up in the great cobbled courtyard. Dare she move nearer? No, better not, she didn't want the archers shooting her down, fair game, in the bright moonlight.

There was Wizard strutting among them, resplendent in purple robes, and giving his orders, no doubt. Wacky grumbled to herself, she couldn't hear, from this distance; she and Puss must do a bit of reconnoitring tomorrow.

Gosh, Wizard was handing out parcels to the servants. She shivered, she bet those parcels didn't contain lovely gifts. Ah, a bit of action now. All the servants were dispersing. Goodness, gracious! Some of them were making for the woods. Would they go as far as her cave? Probably not as they all feared her and Puss. Wacky thought about him – he could take care of himself; all the same, she had better be off home.

Quickly she sailed through the air, setting all the birds squawking; what was Wacky up to now? Down she plummeted and parked in the thick undergrowth leading to her cave.

'Ah, there you are, Puss! We must stay quiet – Wizard's people are on the prowl!'

The darkness gathered over the wood but no one came near all night. Wacky fell asleep at last, pondering over the parcels – what would be in them?

The following day she and Puss set out on their

reconnaissance. The witch took her broomstick and used it as a walking-stick as they penetrated the thorny bushes of the forest. She wore her dark green cloak and hood, guaranteed to protect her from the thorns. Where the bushes were the thickest she carried her black cat.

'What is in the parcels, Puss?' she rasped.

Puss meditated, 'Poison, I should think, Mistress.'

Wacky shook her head, 'Too obvious, I should think. Wizard would know I wouldn't eat food that might hold poison.'

As they came to the end of the forest she whispered, 'Better be careful now, Puss.'

They surveyed the courtyard; all was quiet, eerily quiet, not an archer could be seen. How surprising! But they were there somewhere, she was sure.

'We'll have to come again when it's dark, Puss, and have a look at the fields round the castle. Somehow I don't think the parcels were placed in the woods. Methinks the servants were afraid of me!' She cackled away, quite pleased with the idea. 'Best go home now and have our dinner – it's delicious trout today my love.'

Wacky was pleased no one had invaded her domain, surrounded as it was with prickly bushes. Wizard must entice her out, surely, if he were to wreak revenge.

Up in the castle Wicked Wizard smiled with satisfaction. How he was going to enjoy life. What fun the parcels contained! The Witch must have no idea what he had planned! She hadn't appeared on her broomstick since his servants had placed their parcels so strategically!

That was a bit strange, he thought, suddenly; she must be holed-up in the place she called home. Funny how he had never found where she lived. Had she put a magic circle round it too? Never mind, he was going to get his own back soon. He sighed with satisfaction as he plumped up his pillows and lay down to rest on his thorn-free bed.

The forest was quiet; all the birds were fast asleep, but slowly and stealthily Wacky and Puss climbed onto the broomstick. Only a tweet or two marked their ascent into the air and soon they were soaring high above the trees en route for the castle.

Over the fields they flew. 'Can you see any parcels Puss?' cried Wacky.

'Not yet,' he purred.

They circled round and round, diving low only to find stones instead of parcels. 'Let's try another site.' Wacky piloted her broomstick further afield, and then she saw one. 'Success,' she shouted gleefully. 'Success at last Puss!'

Dare she land? Were the archers or foes in hiding?

'I will scout around,' mewed Puss, and lightly he sprang off the broomstick. No one noticed the low black shape moving purposefully over the grass and certainly no one saw him crouching low over the prize.

He sniffed the parcel and tugged at the loose string. The paper fell off revealing a square cardboard box. He sniffed again at the contents, all brightly coloured. Whatever were they?

He miaowed to Wacky to come nearer and she hovered above avidly, viewing the contents. Could she land?

'Puss, scout around again – I'm going to land!'

'Right, Mistress, no one is about, hurry down.'

80

Wacky jumped off and picked up the box. Puss and she settled themselves on the broomstick and, in a trice, they were off. But they were not unseen. Wicked Wizard was at his window, telescope in hand. How he smiled! Wacky couldn't hide her curiosity, she simply had to see what was in the box! Yawning happily, he fell asleep.

They all slept late. Wacky was awakened by Puss miaowing for his breakfast, so late this morning. His mistress stoked up the fire to cook her own in a black frying-pan. She had a nice slice of ham with mushrooms she had gathered from the fields. The birds had been up long ago and one or two hopped by hoping for a crumb or two.

Replete, Wacky's thoughts turned to the box. 'Come and see, Puss. Aren't these things nice and gaudy, and they are all funny shapes!'

'What's that long thing, Mistress? A little broomstick?'

'Mmm, that does look so,' replied the Witch. 'Funny, how other boxes were placed in the fields as well. To make sure I found one at least, I suppose, eh? I wonder what it is all about!'

She cradled the long thing in her arms. Puss sat on her knee to get a better look, and suddenly, whoosh! Up in the air they went! A spark from the fire had ignited the rocket.

Just in the nick of time, Wacky caught hold of the branches of a tree and it wove a protective screen of leaves about her and Puss. There, right on top, she sat with Puss still clinging on for dear life!

Way up in the castle the Wizard laughed and laughed. He knew, didn't he, he just knew Wacky couldn't help

poking about, but this beat all! The box of fireworks would, sooner or later, be set alight and show him where Wacky lived; but this was too, too funny for words! Tomorrow they would set off the fireworks in the other boxes to celebrate.

'Oh, what shall we do, Puss,' cried Wacky. 'My broomstick is down below in the cave. Whatever shall I do without it? And the Wizard will be sending his servants and his archers any minute now.'

'Don't fret, Mistress,' mewed her cat, 'I will streak down below and bring it up to you right away.'

'Mind you don't fall, Puss,' shouted Wacky as Puss slid from branch to branch skilfully.

In no time at all Puss was back with the magic broomstick and Wacky smiled with relief.

All the time she had been thinking hard. 'Come near, Puss,' she whispered. 'I'll put a spell on this tree and we will all move to another wood.'

The tree listened. He had been living in this wood for years and years and, more importantly, he was in love with the tree alongside. Such a lovely lady tree!

Alarmed, he felt he had to speak to this domineering Witch. 'Please, Wacky, put a spell on my lady friend; I can't go anywhere without her. I shall just fade away and die!'

Wacky was amazed to hear the tree speaking; she made up her mind at once. 'That shall be so, dear tree. Tomorrow is Midsummer's Day and, every following year, you and your love will be able to move wherever you fancy!'

'Seems a very good deal, my dear,' spoke Wacky's tree.

84

'Tomorrow, then, away we go – I fancied a change, didn't you, my love?'

During the night, Wizard's servants and the archers came to find the Witch's cave, but they got covered with thorns and prickles. Wacky and Puss chuckled away, safe in their tree!

Midsummer's Day dawned with pouring rain, and it turned out to be a damp squib! The fireworks were nearly all sodden!

Nowhere could Wacky be found and, secretly, the Wizard missed chasing her!

Later, he gazed at the empty space where once two lovely forest trees bloomed. 'It's all Wacky's doing,' he mourned. 'Where has she gone with her dratted cat?' He missed her!

The Swallow's Return

It was a lovely balmy day in April, and Sammy Swallow had just returned from his winter sojourn in Africa.

With what joy he had flown unerringly towards the gabled white-washed farm set in miles of fertile fields. Would the old nest be still there, safe and comfy high up on the rafters of the barn? Would his parents be there? If so, it was up to him to find a partner and they would build a nest together. Smoothly he negotiated the small entrance at the top of the big barn door, and he tweeted a song of greeting.

The hay smelled sweet, and he heard faint mewings from somewhere, in a corner. New life! Sammy was full of joy and flew up to the rafters. The nest he had left last autumn was still there and empty. Would it do if he found someone to build a life with? Well, she would decide.

He rested for a while and watched as a girl came through the little door carrying a saucerful of milk for proud pussy with her four kittens. A farmer's boy took a forkful or two of hay, glancing up as Sammy, beady-eyed looked him over.

'Aha,' he cried, 'back home are you? You are the leader, you're first!'

Sammy smoothed his feathers, dark brown shot through

with a lovely midnight blue sheen, pride and contentment washing over him. He slept. Safely cocooned within the walls of his birthplace he stayed still, his feathers at rest after carrying him safely over a thousand and more miles on the return journey.

A soft whirring movement awakened him, and he looked around; there perching on the rim of the nest, was Susie!

'My dear,' he trilled, 'I wondered if I would ever see you again!'

Susie's eyes sparkled. 'Hello, Sammy, I've been looking all over for you. I got back yesterday and found the nests empty; I thought I must have got the wrong farm, and got so upset wondering where you were – and your parents and mine!'

So Sammy wasn't the first back! 'How did you manage to be first back, Susie?'

'To tell you the truth, Sammy, I got a lift!'

'How?'

'I was blown off course over the Sahara Desert; I was so tired and weary and below me was the sea going on and on for ever. I was weak from lack of food and fighting the wind, but then I saw a lovely big ship below. I plummeted down and landed in a little boat. I found myself a cosy spot out of the wind. The next thing I knew was the ship was still. I looked about me and saw and heard the sights and sounds of dear old England. I fed on scraps lying about and was soon myself again, and I soared up in the air to start my journey home; I tasted once again the delectable English insects!'

Sammy looked at her with adoring eyes. 'How brave

and clever you are my love; let us spend some time together celebrating our return, and then make a nest!'

'Oh, Sammy, that will be just lovely. We can make some chicks, and then journey together to Africa in the autumn!'

For a day or two, the lovebirds circled the farm, revelling in the sights of home and visiting their friends who nested in outhouses. Everywhere was blooming and blossoming. Trees pink and white, and hedgerows and fields dotted with daisies, dandelions and clover.

'Where shall we make our home, Susie?' They were taking a few moments' rest, and were perched on the gable-end of the farmhouse.

'Here, Sammy, we can look out over the fields, it's so open, not like the barn. There's this magnificent tree casting shade in the heat of summer, but not too close so predators can stretch out and reach our nest, and I love to smell the sweet roses climbing up the wall,' she finished.

'Just as you wish, my dear, we will begin our work tomorrow.' And they both soared up in the air to catch some succulent insects, so plentiful near the farm.

How lovely it was to snuggle up together in the old nest and wake to the comforting sounds of the animals of the farm. The hay smelled sweet and Flossie was busy washing her kittens, who mewed constantly.

It was time for breakfast, and Sammy and Susie streaked out through the top of the big barn door, and soared high in the air to catch some juicy flies. Over the fields they flew and, to their delight, they came across their parents on the last leg of their journey from Africa.

After much tweeting they all flew into the barn; it was clear now that Susie and Sammy must build their own nest. There was no time like the present! Off they went towards the farmhouse; they inspected the site and chose a snug place high up between two windows. The aspect was good, and nearby was the trellis of roses which Susie so adored. The big oak tree stood nearby with its protective branches which would provide welcome shade in the summer months.

'Let us fly to the pond and make a firm foundation with mud pellets,' cried Sammy.

The water was pretty, backed by irises which would flower by the by. Sammy and Susie delighted in collecting the mud in such idyllic surroundings; it was quite some time since they had alighted there. Now it was their turn to build a wonderful nest. Busily they moulded the pellets and carried them back to the farmhouse; there they prodded them into place under the eaves.

What hard work it was! From time to time they soared high above revelling in the day's blue skies and gentle breeze. Spring was here and the earth warming, and the trees and flowers were budding.

'Where shall we go for straw?' wondered Sammy, 'We will need to weave it carefully to make a good strong nest.'

'I know the very place,' smiled Susie. 'In the far field there is a thing right in the middle. I thought the farmer was standing there, but he never moved, so I investigated. It's something like a man and he wears overalls and a funny straw hat. Straw sticks out from his arms and legs. I'm sure we could pull out a few nice lengths.'

'It's a scarecrow, Susie. He's supposed to frighten us off the fields so we don't eat the grain!'

'But we eat insects,' said she, 'and it didn't frighten me!'

'Let's go right now,' shrieked Sammy, and off they went.

Susie perched on the hat as Sammy tugged at the straw. She peered into the face and admitted he did look like a man when seen at close quarters. When Sammy had a load, she plucked grasses from the hedgerows and off they darted to weave them around the mud pellets.

'I think that's all for today,' trilled Sammy, 'I'm exhausted!'

'So am I,' tweeted Susie. 'We'll begin again tomorrow. It's firm, and shouldn't fall even if the wind blows.'

As they left the farmhouse the farmer's wife looked up. 'The swallows are back, Joe, I think they are nesting with us this spring.'

That night Susie and Sammy snuggled up in their cosy nest. True, it wasn't quite finished, but its foundation was nice and secure.

'It's grand being able to peep out over the fields, isn't it Sammy and just think, in the summer the pink roses will waft their perfume over us and give us sweet dreams!'

Sammy smiled, he liked to indulge his lady-love and what suited Susie, suited him!

Early next morning our two were back at work relieving poor old scarecrow of a few more lengths of straw which they cunningly wove in and out of the moulded pellets of mud. Susie plaited the grasses, and there it was, all done, their lovely nest which would soon be filled with lovely smooth white eggs. Susie couldn't wait to be mother and see their fluffy chicks!

Then came carefree days, dipping and diving over the fields and hedges till Susie relaxed and didn't want to wander far from home. Soon four white eggs lay in the nest and Sammy, very importantly, flew hither and thither for tempting insects to fortify Susie for her long vigil on the eggs.

She didn't stir from the nest except on rare occasions as Sammy wasn't as well equipped as she was for keeping the eggs at just the right temperature.

Came the special day! One skinny baby swallow erupted from the shell. What a to-do! Word spread around and, before long, grandparents arrived to congratulate the young couple!

When the four eggs had hatched Susie was beside herself, and Sammy was bursting with pride; mind you he didn't consider them as beautiful as their mother did! Perhaps when they were covered with fluffy feathers they might be pretty! But, wisely, he kept his thoughts to himself!

Long days and nights feeding the ever-open mouths! The parents were just about exhausted, and they longed for the day when the chicks would leave the nest. Then Susie worried about them falling!

'They must be good and ready, Sammy, before they go. They simply must be able to fly straight away!'

'I know, my love, but don't fret, they are strong and have watched us flying. Instinct will take over, just you see.'

Susie wasn't so sure but, one glorious happy day, the

93

chicks were tired of peeping over the nest and one venturous baby darted out. She'd seen her mother encouraging her from the oak tree. It looked so attractive with its pretty green foliage, and mother was there, wasn't she? Off the chick flew and, encouraged by their sister's venture, the other three followed suit!

What a great day! The chicks played hide-and-seek among the branches but, at nightfall, they all came back to the safety of the nest.

The following days were glorious. The parents took their family over the fields and up, up to the heavens to partake of choice insects. Then came the night when Susie and Sammy were alone once more; they had done their work, the chicks were fully fledged and away.

As summer sunshine gilded the farmhouse, the oak tree cast a protective shade over the eaves, and Sammy and Susie were grateful for it as the profusion of leaves fanned them on the hot summer evenings. The roses were a riot of colour and scent, and the days were long and happy for them, grandparents and their friends.

But the summer couldn't last for ever. Hay-making time was over, and what a commotion that caused, with the fields filled with people gathering in the hay. Someone took down Mr Scarecrow and bits of straw and grasses flew about the field.

Slowly the days were shortening, and the swallows began to murmur among themselves. They took to gathering in the skies and whirring around in a dark cloud like flies.

The farmer looked up. 'Mary,' he said, 'it won't be long before our little visitors leave us to winter abroad.'

'Yes,' she smiled, 'I'll miss their darting about the place, and there will be no more chirping under the eaves. Lovely the way they chose to summer with us – they must have fancied the roses!'

'Don't be daft, woman,' he grunted; but she was so right.

Susie and Sammy told their chicks about the flight they would be taking. The birds were young and eager to experience this new adventure. Long days on the wing had strengthened them, and they were ready for the off.

'See how they are gathering, Joe. Are they plotting their course?'

'Don't know, Mary. I guess they go by some special instinct, but they always gather a few weeks before the start.'

'Perhaps they have a leader,' laughed she.

'Could be, could be,' answered Joe.

One morning they were gone, bright and early. How quiet now seemed the farm, the barn and the outbuildings. Time to gather the rest of the harvest and prepare for winter.

Sammy, Susie and their chicks joined up with the family and friends and set off for the warmer shores of Africa. It was good going over England, and they made excellent time across the Channel. How amazed the chicks were at the sight of the sea and the boats upon it. They looked with awe at the blue-grey expanse, and remembered Susie's adventure in the spring. But they were strong, they could soar and dive endlessly.

The flock of birds streamed on purposefully over the

95

flat terrain of northern France, seeking marshy stretches at night where they could safely renew their strength and obtain good food. Sammy and Susie knew their chicks were vigorous and eager for this long adventure, but they were a bit concerned for their grandparents. They were finding it hard to keep up. Would they be able to reach their goal in the sunny haven of Africa? Time would tell. One thing was certain, the cold winds and snows of England were not an option for them.

At break of day the swallows moved on. Most found the journey effortless – they had got well into the rhythm of it all. The sun was shining ever brighter as they reached the south of France. Lovely palm trees fanned the air, and oh, the flowers! Extravagant colours with heavenly scents delighted the chicks and revived the flagging spirits of the older birds.

The young birds were spellbound with the brightness of it all. Couldn't they stay? Why journey on? Surely they had gone far enough? Gently their parents explained that swallows had always chosen western Africa for their sojourn. It was perfect with luscious insects, and no mistral wind which was the nuisance of southern France. However, the grandparents had had enough journeying, and they elected to stay.

With hurried goodbyes the flock went on its way crossing the Mediterranean Sea, ready for the formidable journey across the Sahara Desert. Now the chicks could see why their grandparents had stayed behind. They hoped this new place their parents had mapped out for them was worthy of all their effort!

How long would it last, this soulless journey in dry,

hot air? How thankful they were at night to rest in an oasis their parents had discovered long ago. They would make a point of remembering it too! On and on they travelled; the farm swallows were now alone. Not many remained of the starter flock, they had all dispersed. Africa was big! There were lots of ideal places near the coast with lush vegetation and very big juicy insects!

'Won't be long now!' Susie tweeted to her four chicks.

'What are these domes?' cried one.

'They're mud huts with straw roofs.'

'Gosh what a lot of nests they would make,' chirruped another.

Already they had sampled the delicious new flies. It was like being given an expensive box of chocolates!

'Not far now,' encouraged Father, 'I can smell the sea not too far away over there.'

'Here we are,' cried Susie. 'See the cluster of trees and the vivid flowers growing in that marsh; it's just perfect!'

The family glided down, revelling in the warm damp air, and knowing that the long journey was finally over safely.

'See,' cried one of their brood, 'there's one of those big nests of straw over there!' Sammy and Susie laughed delightedly.

So passed long days exploring the great forests and the wonderful coastline. They revelled in the salty air of the sea and would soar and dive over the rocky cliffs. Flying over the vast plain, they came across other swallows fresh from England, and they all had joyous reunions. Africa was so big, and they only discovered a tiny part of it. They marvelled at the gigantic river with its ever-

97

plunging waterfalls and here they fraternised with the African swallows who made their nests on the riverbank.

Life was one long holiday, and the chicks were overcome with excitement. Sammy and Susie wondered how their parents were faring in the south of France. Maybe they would make it their permanent home. Nesting was no longer a priority.

But as the weeks became months, Sammy and Susie became restless; the call of their English home was becoming stronger. They longed for the warm days with cool breezes and April showers. They yearned for the farmhouse and the old barn. Susie's eyes sparkled as she thought of rearing still more chicks. And wasn't it splendid, making a nest with Sammy! Their growing chicks too were filled with the age-old instinct to mate and to breed.

All at once the swallows began gathering in the skies. Others came from further down the coast and, delightedly, Sammy and family joined in the glorious reunion. Fresh and full of vigour they contemplated their journey home. Once over the Sahara Desert there shouldn't be many problems.

By now the chicks were highly independent and they were first to fly off from the main group of swallows. 'See you at the farm,' they cried happily. Susie wasn't a bit pleased. She wanted to protect them from dangers she and Sammy were all too well aware of.

The first stage led them to a lovely oasis and there she was relieved to find her chicks. They had remembered, she smiled. Then came the long flight up to the sea crossing.

'Wasn't it around here you took a lift, Susie?'

'A bit further on, Sammy. Oh, I do hope our young ones don't lose their way; they should have kept with us, Sammy!'

'Let's veer to the west a little,' said Sammy; 'there's a stopping-place not as big as an oasis, but there is water and a few bushes for shelter.'

So they rested, and felt quite refreshed as they approached the sea. Far below sailed the little ships and boats, the sun glinting on the water.

'I wonder where our parents are Sammy? Do you think we could stop off and find them?'

'I don't think it's a good idea, Susie. We have still a long way to go and you are tired already. We will go in the autumn – how about that?'

Susie agreed, perhaps they would have news of them when they got back home to the farm. Other swallows might know.

So they crossed over the Mediterranean, and began the next stage of their journey. Way in the distance were the snow-clad peaks of the Pyrenees, so they knew they were well on their way home. Over farmland and winding rivers, with a castle or two perched on high land, they flew. Then across the Channel, and there was the wonderful sight of the white cliffs of England.

There was no need to rest now as relief and joy swept over them – they were in sight of home. There was the lovely farmhouse with the trellis of roses, sleeping before it burst into bloom in June. Streaking over the garden they flew unerringly into their cosy nest. Oh, how lovely to be back home!

100

After an idyllic night's rest, they thought about their young ones. Were they home? After soaring high for a delicious breakfast of flies – oh how superior were the farm insects! – Sammy and Susie flew into the barn. The nests were all empty.

'Oh, Sammy, oh Sammy,' screeched Susie, 'what has happened to our chicks?'

'Now, now, Susie, they will be back soon, you see. They probably didn't take the direct route and our little short cuts.'

But Susie was inconsolable as they circled round the farm buildings asking friends if they had seen their brood.

'We saw them flying over the Mediterranean, Susie. Sandy and I were having a bit of a spree circling the boats and, at one time, they were with us.'

'Little beggars,' grunted their father, 'they never gave a thought to us worrying.'

Susie was a little mollified. 'So tomorrow they might be here Sammy?'

'Of course, my dear, of course.'

But tomorrow came with no news. What a long day it was! Where were the chicks, and how were the grandparents faring? Susie was quite overcome by it all.

But the long day ended and, wonder of wonders, bright and early the following morning, they were wakened by two little swallows chirruping a happy 'Good morning!'

'Oh how pleased we are to see you,' cried Susie and Sammy. 'Where have you been all this time, and where are the other two?'

'They went off to find Grannie and Grandpa!'

'Oh, my,' worried Susie; 'they must have got lost.'

101

'Now, now, Susie,' remonstrated Sammy, 'when they come back to us they will be able to tell you all about how well your parents are, living in the south of France. I'm sure they won't have lost their way – not *our* chicks!'

'And where have you two been?' Susie wanted to hear all about it.

A bit shamefaced the chicks told of their fun around the boats. Susie relaxed, worn out by the excitement and worry.

'Perhaps our wandering young ones will stay there for ever,' grumbled Susie.

'I doubt it,' answered Sammy. 'I think they will come home eventually to mate and have chicks of their own.'

And he was so right; one glorious morning the errant chicks flew into the old barn to smell again the sweet hay, but also to pick the site for their own nests. Then on to the farmhouse to see Sammy and Susie, but they were out over the fields to see if another Mr Scarecrow could provide them with straw. Yes, there he was, all spruce and smiling!

It was by the pond that the family reunion took place. The water was clear and unsullied with tall grasses and irises making a pretty picture. Up in the air they all soared, happy and free.

Yes, Grannie and Grandpa were well, among the palm trees of southern France.

As they flew back to the farm, Joe looked up. 'The swallows are with us again, Mary.'

'Aye,' said Mary, 'and they've brought the family with them too!'

That night everyone was happy in the old barn and

at the farmhouse. Susie snuggled up to Sammy, dreaming of the new nest they would make. Just think, they would be grandparents too! Her eyes sparkled; all was well, the family was home.

104

Bessie and Billie Duck Go Downriver

Bessie Duck awoke to a fine day. She fluffed up her soft brown feathers and looked around for her partner, Billie Drake. He wasn't there! Neither were the sheltering reeds and grasses of home in the sleepy marsh with its slow-moving waters.

There was water everywhere, simply everywhere! And it was moving fast too. How come she was not caught up in the flow?

She looked around. During the night the waters had carried her down to the river, but a fallen tree had diverted the flow, making a little pond just for her! So that was why she had slept so well. Just like home!

But where was Billie? It was lonely here. She peeped through the blackened branches of the tree, and shuddered.

Bessie had never ever seen so much water, and there was no one on it either. It stretched for miles and miles. No stately white swan appeared, no dabbling ducks – no Billie.

She called with a loud harsh quack, but no soft answering queek sounded over the vast expanse of water. Bessie looked up at the sky. If only a flight of geese would pass over, she could ask them to find Billie.

What should she do? She was oh, so hungry. She scanned the water but only leaves and twigs marred its surface. The sun had not yet come out and there was nothing to attract juicy flies such as formed part of breakfast in the marsh.

Bessie was just about to upend when a slight movement on the branch alerted her. With a lightning strike she seized a small dark frog cunningly concealed in the fork of the branch. She swallowed; ah that was better. With her beak she probed the soft rotting wood and added a mouthful of succulent insects to her diet. All was not lost; there was life after the flood!

For the rest of that day Bessie was content with her little backwater. She swam to the bank and muddy edges of the surrounding field. Worms were aplenty with one or two slugs for interest! Also, she feasted on a few grains left over from harvesting.

As nightfall cast shadows over the gently moving water, she felt quite tired. Such an exciting day, but she felt quite pleased with the outcome. She slept, lulled by the gentle lapping of the water. Bessie felt quite secure, she had sense enough to find shelter the other side of the branch. Who knows – a dog might hurtle over the field and find her! Cats were so different, no sailors they!

Bessie awoke to a grand new day showing blue skies and a watery sun. This time there was great excitement. A boat actually sailed by! Men in yellow oilskins manned it and they seemed in a hurry. Off they surged, sending a great wave which buffeted Bessie this way and that till she was swept from her sheltered lake and right into the main highway of water.

Oh, she didn't like it one bit! She tumbled swiftly

downriver and it quite took her breath away. Was she alone on this breakneck water-chute? She hadn't time to look around, she was concerned with surviving. Oh, horrors! Would there be a waterfall at the end of this ride, or the canal locks she had heard so much about? Where was Billie? She missed him so.

Vaguely she sensed that fields no longer hugged the water. There was a house, and another – and another! The river was narrowing too and she was so glad not to be in the centre of all that terrifying water. She could see people lining the bank. Oh, good, life was becoming normal again!

There was a majestic swan honking gently, its plumage white and beautiful. She must try to aim for the bank, there she would feel so safe with a swan as a protecting shield. Valiantly she struggled against the flow and came at last to the safety of the overhanging bushes and reeds.

'Hi, there,' hoo-hoed Susie Swan, 'come far?'

Bessie was only too delighted to tell all to this sympathetic Queen of Birds.

'My, you have travelled far,' sympathised Susie, 'it's a shame about your partner, but never mind, I'm sure we'll all meet up again eventually! My partner is just foraging for food; he's not far away – just by the bridge.'

After a while, as Bessie rested from her ordeal, the stately white swan emerged from under the bridge and made towards them. In his beak he carried a crust of bread someone had thrown to him. Oh, she was hungry! Could she, perhaps, have a crumb or two?

'Here is my friend, Bessie Duck, Charlie. She's had such a terrifying journey from her home in Buttercup

Marsh. I'll just give her a little piece of the bread you've so kindly brought for me!'

Charlie made a slight honk and Susie and Bessie settled down to enjoy their meal.

For the rest of the day the three rested, but Charlie foraged for tasty worms for their evening meal.

Bessie went to sleep that night with one wondering eye on the bright golden lights lining the riverbank. What a wonderful world it was!

Morning came and with it torrents of rain. The waters were choppy and Bessie was terrified she might get swept downstream again.

'Are you all right, Bessie Duck?' honked Susie. 'Hide behind me!'

Charlie sailed up to add his support. 'Don't be afraid little duck. The storms will pass and then I'll go downstream to find Billie Drake for you!'

Bessie stopped shuddering and, feeling comforted, she fell asleep. She woke to find the river calm and peaceful. Blue skies filled the heavens and there by her side was her dear friend, Susie.

'Here are come worms for you, Bessie. Had a nice sleep then? Charlie has gone to find your Billie!'

'Oh, what a good swan he is,' quacked Bessie.

'I know,' answered Susie spreading her snow-white feathers in a beautiful display.

Little boats had taken to the water and were ferrying people up and down the river.

'I think,' honked Susie, 'that the waters flooded the people's homes. Look how the boats are full of clothes and boxes and things.'

So she wasn't the only one upset by the storm, thought Bessie. How many other ducks had been swept away too? What about her neighbours in Buttercup Marsh? Still, her main concern was Billie. Oh, *where* was he?

It seemed ages before Charlie came back, but Billie wasn't with him. Oh, dear, where *was* Billie?

Don't you fret! Billie was way back home near Buttercup Marsh. When the storm blew up and the rain poured down, Billie was swept away from Bessie. Try as he may, he couldn't stay by her side among the dark green rushes. Oh, how he did his utmost to recover from each buffeting of the waves and wind, and swim back to her, but, alas, Bessie was suddenly free of the protective circle of rushes and she was carried downstream at an alarming pace.

His dear beloved Bessie! Amazing that she didn't even quack in response to his soft queek. Still, they had been on a long visit upstream, yesterday, to where her parents lived near Daisy Brook. They had both been very tired last night.

Billie was hit by a vicious gust of wind which swept him right up the bank. Dazed and muddy, he had enough sense to waddle a few feet away from the surging waters, impatient to claim him again. Breathless, he sank down on the soft grass and gazed up at the lowering clouds in the night sky.

A fleeting thought that he might be at the mercy of a dog or cat in this open field flashed across his mind, before he fell fast asleep. When he awoke, all was quiet. Gosh, he'd been lucky – here he was in an open field with no cover at all! He shook his feathers, happy to find he was none the worse for his little adventure.

109

Then realisation swept over him. Bessie wasn't here, oh dear! Everything else was forgotten as he waddled over to the bank and searched the rushes but, of course, she couldn't be here. Hadn't he seen her floating headlong down the swollen river?

'Bessie,' he queeked, but there was no reply save the gurgle of the waters now at peace. No sign of life, no waterfowl, not even a bird in the sky. He felt so forlorn and unhappy. But he must go and look for Bessie after he'd fortified himself with some worms.

Then he set sail down the vast expanse of water, not a bit intimidated by its size, so worried was he for Bessie's safety. It was amazing that there was no one about, the silence was uncanny.

Eventually, he spied the little pond which had been a haven for Bessie, and he decided to spend the night there. As he made himself comfortable among the fallen twigs and branches, he spied it – one magic brown feather, Bessie's feather! Comforted and happy, he nestled it among his own and slept a deep and restorative sleep. He was on the trail! He would find her!

With the morning sun shedding a lambent glow over the water, he partook of his breakfast. He too spied the rotting wood with insects aplenty. He smiled; he knew Bessie would have found these delicacies! As he ate, the boat with yellow-clad men swept downriver and Billie moved hurriedly into the shelter of the fallen tree. A flock of geese arrowed across the sky, trumpeting glad cries, and suddenly life seemed normal once more.

He set sail down the narrowing river, noting the houses lining the bank and quite a few people walking along. There was great activity, with doors wide open and stacks of boxes, carpets and things being pulled out. It seemed quite apparent; the river had burst its banks and surged into people's homes during the nightmare storm.

Brightly coloured boats were being loaded up with neighbours and their possessions. The river was so crowded, but Billie steered expertly between it all and caught bits of bread and cake thrown especially for him!

But where was Bessie? He scanned the waters but only saw a swan, honking in a little backwater.

Further downstream he saw a swan; you couldn't miss him with his dazzling white plumage. But Charlie missed Billie. In the shadow of a long boat, the little duck merged with the dark water, and he sailed on and on.

As the light dimmed and night fell, Billie needed to find a haven – a little backwater surrounded by reeds and grasses, just as he had enjoyed way back in Buttercup Marsh.

The river seemed pretty normal now. People had gone from the banks and there were no houses. Where could he sleep? He was getting so tired, he *must* stop before long.

Just as he was feeling so forlorn and dispirited, there was a loud noise, a flurry of brown and white wings, and a flock of geese landed on the water and surrounded Billie.

'Hi there, Billie, whatever are you doing so far from home? Where's Bessie?'

The little drake felt quite overwhelmed and, after surviving all his trouble alone, the kindness and friendliness threatened to make him weep. He pulled himself together and fluffed his feathers.

'I've lost my Bessie; I've not seen her since the flooding in Buttercup Marsh. I'm so upset' – and here his queek wobbled – 'and I've nowhere to spend the night!'

'Never mind,' trumpeted Gertie Goose, 'we'll take you to a nice place. We're settling down ourselves and you'll be so safe with us.'

So, with an escort of eight Canada geese, Billie swam a bit further down the river and there, under a bridge, was a creek wonderfully sheltered from the river traffic. Immediately he fell asleep, comforted by the sound of the soft trumpeting of his friends the Canada geese.

He awoke to a bright new day and, at first, wondered where on earth he was. Gerald Goose was around in a flash, offering some succulent worms.

'Where are you off to, Gerald?' queeked Billie.

'Oh, not very far away, we're based at a bird sanctuary, a few miles downriver. It's a great place to be, Billie – wonderful friends and tasty food. Idyllic in fact.'

'Could Bessie have travelled so far, do you think?'

'No,' said Gerald, sadly. 'It's way off the river; she would need to fly over the big wide road which is very dangerous.' He considered. 'How is her flying, Billie?'

'So-so,' admitted he. 'If you fellows surged ahead, I'm sure she could put on a spurt if necessary and not be frightened by the roar of the traffic. But she's not here, Gerald, oh I *am* worried!'

'Do you think you could have passed her, Billie?' asked Gertie, overhearing the conversation.

'Surely not,' he queeked, 'but there was a lot of

confusion way back with people and boats – could I?' His eyes lit up. Perhaps he *had* passed Bessie!

'Let's sail back up river,' trumpeted Gertie and Gerald, 'come on!'

With hope renewed the trio swam happily upstream. Halfway there they came upon Charlie Swan.

'Hi there, is your name Billie Drake?' he honked. 'Do you know Bessie Duck?'

'Do I know Bessie Duck?' queeked Billie. 'Where is she, oh where *is* she? Is she all right?'

'Right as rain,' honked Charlie, 'just half a mile upstream; she's with my partner Susie in a lovely backwater.'

Billie splashed happily upstream at a terrific speed. Accompanying him with leisurely strokes were his friends Gertie and Gerald and Charlie Swan!

Bessie was the first to spy Billie. 'Billie,' she quacked. 'Billie where *have* you been?'

'Where have *you* been, my love!' queeked he.

Such a sweet reunion and a sharing of worms, bread and grains for a midday feast.

Late into the evening Bessie and Billie relived the events of the past few days.

'Oh, what a long way we've wandered from home,' queeked Billie.

'It's far too long to go back,' answered Bessie, 'and all our friends in Buttercup Marsh, where are they?'

'We think,' honked Gertie and Gerald, overhearing the last remark, 'you would be well advised to come with us, to Bright and Beautiful Bird Sanctuary, we're all no happy there.'

'How come you are upriver then?' queeked Billie Drake.

'Just a little holiday, that's all, and to revisit old haunts.'

'What do you think, Bessie?'

'I'm willing it you are, dear Billie.'

So it was settled; with the dawn Gertie and Gerald Goose would accompany Billie and Bessie on their journey to the bird sanctuary. Night fell, with Bessie and Billie snuggled up together among the reeds of the river bank.

Morning came, with a soft fine mist shrouding the sun and, after a breakfast of lovely worms, the four set off in perfect weather.

'Goodbye, Susie and Charlie Swan,' quacked Bessie.

'Goodbye,' queeked Billie, 'what true friends you are.'

'Sorry we won't be travelling with you, Bessie and Billie,' honked Charlie, 'Susie has to take it easy, you know,' and here he fluffed out his feathers importantly. 'We're expecting cygnets before long.'

'Oh, how marvellous,' and Bessie rushed to rub beaks with her dearest friend, Susie. 'Bye now, take care!'

With promises to return and see the lovely new babies, Bessie and Billie started on their long journey.

At last they came to the motorway, oh what a noise and how fearful it looked with its wide carriageway! Bessie swam closer to Billie, and trembled. 'Don't worry, my love,' he queeked.

Gertie and Gerald left the river and waddled up the bank with its grasses and wild flowers. Bessie and Billie followed rather apprehensively. The noise grew to a roar and the draught caused by the flow of traffic was

114

frighteningly close – and strong. It seemed like a hurricane to the two little ducks.

'Wait for a gap in the traffic,' honked Gerald Goose. So they waited and waited. At long last the traffic abated.

'*Now*,' honked Gerald and off the two flew, followed by Bessie and Billie.

'Oh, Billie,' she quacked, 'oh, Billie!'

'Never fear, Bessie,' he queeked. 'Keep close to me!'

They were over one lane, but the far bank looked awfully far away.

'I'm dropping, Billie, I'm dropping,' she quacked.

'No, you're not, Bessie; come on, not much further, keep it up!'

As Bessie neared the far bank she did indeed plummet, but Gertie Goose saw her fall and honked for Gerald's assistance. The two chivvied and pushed Bessie to safety just in the nick of time as a big car threatened to sweep her under its wheels.

Bessie sank down onto the soft grasses and dandelions. Billie was all overwrought with the trauma of it all. 'All right Bessie, my love?' He rested beside her while Gerald and Gertie waddled off to find some energising food.

The traffic was roaring again, but Bessie and Billie couldn't care; they were safe and sound. The thought came to Billie that perhaps they would have to wait until the cygnets were quite a bit older and ask Charlie and Susie Swan to come and see them. No way would he ask Bessie to fly over that dreaded motorway!

'Ready for a little walk, Bessie?' asked Gertie. 'It's not much further to the bird sanctuary.'

On the way they came to a nice little pond where

they all splashed happily about before they followed a path leading to the Bright and Beautiful Bird Sanctuary.

'How wonderful,' quacked Bessie as they came onto lots of little paths surrounding water with lovely brown bird-houses.

'Indeed, my dear,' queeked Billie, and their eyes grew bright as they came across dozens of mallards and other ducks of all kinds.

'Hi there, Bessie,' someone quacked a greeting.

'Oh, Billie look, there's Debbie Duck from Buttercup Marsh!'

She swam off to greet her long-lost friend and to catch up on the latest news on the river! Billie was so happy for her and he too found someone he knew.

'We're off to meet up with our Canada geese friends,' honked Gertie and Gerald. 'See you later, Bessie and Billie!'

So it was that the two little ducks reached a safe and wonderful haven. Food and lots of new friends were there for the taking. How lucky they had been to meet up with such wonderful friends as Susie and Charlie Swan and Gertie and Gerald Goose. They had guided them to a wonderful haven. The flood hadn't been so bad after all!